''We can't stay here!''

Tate flashed Maggie a grin and glanced around the barn. "Why not? I'll bring in clean hay and put the blanket on top of it. It'll be like sleeping in a feather bed."

Maggie tried not to imagine sleeping with Tate on a soft, old feather bed. "I'll just take the blanket outside and shake it," she murmured.

"Great." Then he heard a strangled sound coming from Maggie. "What..."

Tate turned around and found himself staring, like Maggie, down the twin barrels of a shotgun...one that was pointed directly at his head.

"You want to tell me who you are?" a steely voice said. "Or should I just go ahead and blow you to kingdom come?"

Dear Reader,

American Romance's tenth-anniversary celebration continues....

For the past three months, we've been bringing you some of your favorite authors, and some brand-new ones, in exciting promotions. In its decade, American Romance has launched the careers of over forty writers and made stars of a dozen more.

Kay Wilding is one of them. After getting her start with another publisher, Kay joined American Romance in 1988 and has since written five novels for the series.

Kay worked as an advertising copywriter, a free-lance writer and a trade-magazine editor. Along with her husband and their daughter and son, she makes her home in Atlanta, Georgia.

We hope you've enjoyed our special tenth-anniversary selections. And we look forward to many more anniversaries of success....

Sincerely,

Debra Matteucci
Senior Editor & Editorial Coordinator

Kay Wilding
DREAM MAKER

Harlequin Books

TORONTO • NEW YORK • LONDON
AMSTERDAM • PARIS • SYDNEY • HAMBURG
STOCKHOLM • ATHENS • TOKYO • MILAN
MADRID • WARSAW • BUDAPEST • AUCKLAND

Published October 1993

ISBN 0-373-16508-0

DREAM MAKER

Chapter One

"A double bourbon," Tate Rabun said to the bartender, raising his voice to make himself heard above the ear-splitting din of conversation, raucous laughter and the nasal, twangy sound of Willie Nelson blaring from a jukebox turned up as loud as it would go. "And water on the side," he added.

He was firing for effect tonight, but the water might come in handy as a chaser. He couldn't remember the last time he'd drunk hard liquor straight.

"What brand?" the bartender asked, projecting his voice with practiced ease as he gave a halfhearted swipe at the battered bar with a filthy towel.

"House brand's fine," Tate shouted back. "And keep it coming."

The bartender, who looked a lot like Edward G. Robinson except more menacing, nodded. He turned away and was back in an instant with the bourbon and water. "It's pay as you go," he said, eyeing Tate's suit jacket, white shirt and tie with suspicion.

The Green Lantern Grille and Tavern obviously didn't attract many business types, Tate decided. He took a roll of bills from his pocket, peeled off a fifty and plopped it on the cigarette-scarred counter.

The bartender made a lopsided grimace that might have been meant as a smile. It was the first sign of animation Tate had seen on the man's surly face, but the smile would have been more effective if he hadn't been missing one of his front teeth.

"I'll keep an eye out for when you need a refill," the bartender said when he returned with Tate's change.

Instead of replying, Tate lifted the shot of bourbon and drained it, then took a swig of water to cool the fiery path the whiskey made going down his throat. He pushed the empty shot glass back to the bartender without speaking. He probably couldn't have spoken even if he'd wanted to, Tate thought grimly, wondering if his vocal cords would ever be the same again after drinking such rotgut.

The bartender refilled his glass and took several more bills from the stack on the counter. Tate nodded. He was just lifting the glass to his lips again when the jukebox suddenly went silent and a smattering of applause rippled through the smoke-fogged room. He swiveled his creaky bar stool around to see what was going on.

Two men and a woman were climbing onto a small stage he hadn't noticed when he'd first arrived. He watched as one of the men sat down on a battered piano bench in front of an old upright. The other man plucked aimlessly at a guitar without making much sound, while the woman moved to the microphone and started adjusting it.

The two men could have been identical twins, dressed as they were in tight jeans and plaid shirts, their long hair spreading out in all directions beneath broad-brimmed, western-style Stetsons. Tate narrowed his eyes to get a better look at the woman, but he was sitting too far away to make an accurate appraisal of her face.

He had no such problem with her body. It was world-class, all the erotic dreams he'd ever had in his life rolled into one. She wore a simple black dress that wasn't simple on her at all. It clung to every curve, nicked every cranny. And there were plenty of curves and crannies for the black dress to cling to and nick. Her hair was as black as the dress and was in wild disarray around her face, as if she'd just gotten out of bed and hadn't bothered to comb it yet.

But something was wrong. It took Tate a few seconds to figure out what it was. The woman—spectacular as she was in her little black dress—was sleek and sophisticated. Uptown. Her cohorts, on the other hand, were simple country boys. *Hillbillies*, Tate thought to himself, wincing. *Like me*.

Mismatched as they were, they probably weren't much of a band. But then, this wasn't much of a place. As far as Tate was concerned, the only thing it had going for it was that it was on the outskirts of Atlanta, more than fifty miles from his own stomping grounds in North Georgia. The last thing he wanted tonight was to run into somebody he knew.

He planned to get quietly, knee-walking drunk in private.

When the woman finally had the microphone adjusted to the height she wanted, she tapped on it. Nothing. She made a motion to somebody offstage. After a moment, there was a long, loud squeal—like a hog in pain—from the loudspeakers. Some of the customers shouted protests and the squeal gradually died down.

The woman flashed an intimate smile at the mostly male audience. "Hi, guys. And gals," she purred into the microphone. Low and throaty, her voice sent a shiver up Tate's spine. "Welcome to the Green Lantern. I'm Glo-

ria La Grande and these two handsome studs with me..."
She paused a moment for effect, then gave a blatantly
suggestive wink to the audience. "They're my *accompanists.*"

Tate shook his head, grinning in spite of his black
mood. It wasn't so much what Gloria had said but the
way she said it that set the audience to clapping and
whistling in response.

"Let *me* be your accompanist, Gloria!" a young man
in tight jeans and a chest-hugging T-shirt shouted,
jumping to his feet.

"If you *really* want to see a stud in action..." another man shouted, rotating his hips suggestively, "I'm
your man."

"Hold that thought!" Gloria replied, motioning the
guys in her band to start playing. As soon as they did, she
started singing an old favorite, "Stand by Your Man."

The audience whooped and hollered some more, but
Tate soon lost interest. The woman's voice was okay, but
he wasn't here to be entertained. He was here to try to
forget that his own mother and baby brother had betrayed him.

Thinking about that, Tate winced. Then he clenched
his teeth. He might have been able to fight it—or even to
shrug it off—if it were only one of them. But both of
them, conspiring against him? It was too much to bear.
Too much to even think about.

He turned back to his drink, finished it off and motioned to the bartender for another. While he was waiting, Tate loosened his tie and unbuttoned the top button
of his dress shirt. He shimmied out of his suit jacket, then
carefully folded it and placed it on the bar stool next to
his, preparing to get down to some serious drinking.

MAGGIE BENNETT GAVE a mental sigh of regret. As far as she was concerned, the only interesting customer in the room had just turned his back on her. She kept singing because Gloria La Grande—the ridiculous name she'd chosen for herself at this two-bit saloon—couldn't let her audience down. But her heart wasn't in it anymore.

The guy sitting at the bar—the one who'd turned his back on her—must be the record producer her friend had told her was coming to the show tonight. He was the only guy in the audience wearing a suit and tie. She'd hoped to make a good impression on him, hoped to gain a step up in her career. Face it, she'd hoped he would be so taken with her performance that he'd sign her to a fat recording contract on the spot . . . and she'd be on her way to the big time.

Obviously, that wasn't going to happen.

The man was much more interested in the glass of whiskey in front of him than he was in the singer on the stage behind him. She'd probably feel the same way if she were in his place, Maggie thought with a deep sadness that wasn't exactly self-pity, but mighty close to it.

She forced a huge smile and put all her talents into a big finale for the song she was singing. The applause was only mediocre. *Okay,* she thought, it was time for Gloria La Grande to make a grand exit and for somebody else to take her place. Doing voices—imitating other personalities—was more to Maggie's liking anyway. She could shed her own persona and actually feel as if she were somebody else.

She took the microphone off its stand and held it in her hand, close to her mouth. She took a deep breath, flung back her head and tousled her hair at the same time, stretching sensuously. "Dolly's ready, boys," she said in her lowest, sexiest voice. Then she smiled and turned back to the mike with a wicked grin. "'Here you come a-gain...'" she crooned in her best Dolly Parton imitation.

The audience picked up on it immediately, Maggie noted with satisfaction as they grinned, then started clapping their hands in time to the beat of the music. By the time she approached the end of the number, half of them were on their feet, clapping time to the rhythm of the song. When she finally ended, they applauded wildly.

"You're a great audience!" Maggie said sincerely. "And to show you just how much I love you...I'm going to give you what you want. You name it!"

"I wanna be your accompanist!" a man's voice shouted.

"Naugh-ty, naugh-ty," Maggie said saucily, wagging her finger. "We're talking songs here, not life-styles." She was relieved when the audience laughed. Sometimes situations like this could get pretty nasty.

"Anything by Reba McEntire!" someone shouted.

"Patsy Cline!" somebody else said.

"What?" Maggie teased. "No Elvis?"

"You're a woman. You can't do Elvis!"

"Wanna bet?" Maggie shouted back, hiking the tight black dress up above her knees. "You haven't seen Elvis until you're seen *my* Elvis!" She motioned to the piano player and he immediately launched into a spirited rendition of "Don't Be Cruel," while Maggie gyrated her hips in an equally spirited fashion.

The audience went wild. Maggie even got lost in the thing herself, prancing all around the stage, singing in a low, guttural imitation of Elvis.

Out of the corner of her eye, she saw *him* turn around on his stool to take another look at her—the record producer who'd turned his back on her before. *Don't let him intimidate you,* she told herself. *Forget him. Forget the whole damned world and enjoy yourself.*

And she did. For the first time in a long, long time.

THE WOMAN was good. Damn good. Tate wondered why he'd thought her voice was nothing spectacular when she'd first started singing. Maybe it was because that was a few drinks ago ... quite a few drinks ago, he thought with a wry smile.

"Ready for a refill?" the bartender asked.

Tate looked over at his glass. It was empty. Again. "Sure," he said. Then, after the bartender refilled his glass, Tate waved his hand in the general direction of the bills he'd left on the counter. "Help yourself."

"You want me to take out the same tip you told me to take before?" the man asked amiably.

"Sure."

"Thanks."

"My pleasure," Tate said, turning back again to watch the woman singing on the stage. He blinked his eyes a couple of times to clear his vision, and then frowned. Was he mistaken or had his voice sounded slightly blurred just then?

"I hope not," Tate said, testing it.

"Beg pardon?" said the bartender.

"What?" Tate said.

"Did you say something?"

Tate thought for a second. "Oh. I said I hoped I wasn't mistaken." If his voice was starting to become blurred, then he was well on his way to fulfilling his mission of drinking himself into oblivion in order to forget his brother's and mother's betrayal.

The bartender frowned. "About what?"

Tate waved his hand and snickered. "Nothing important."

"I'll be right here if you need anything," the man said.

Tate returned his attention to the singer, squinting one eye to get a better fix on her, but either he had had too much to drink or the haze of blue smoke between them distorted his vision. She was a blur, an erotic blur, a shapely female form in a clingy black dress, with a mass of tangled black hair tumbling around her face.

And Lord, could she sing!

She was imitating Crystal Gayle now, sensuously crooning "Don't It Make My Brown Eyes Blue," while she swayed from side to side and front to back. Suddenly, Tate found himself swaying along with her. He stopped. Then, guiltily glancing around, he saw that every man in the audience was swaying with the singer, too.

What was going on? he wondered fuzzily. Was the singer a temptress? Had she somehow managed to cast a spell over everyone in the place?

Could be, he decided. She was that good.

And that sexy.

But she's not for you, he reminded himself. *Not tonight. You have other plans for tonight.*

Tate frowned, trying to recall what those other plans were. Then painfully, he remembered.

He sighed and lifted his glass to the singer in a silent toast. He had no idea she was watching him but she must have been, because she stopped singing for a moment, touched her fingers to her lips and blew him a kiss across the room.

The audience applauded.

Tate blinked.

Gloria La Grande finished her song and the audience applauded again. She moved across the stage, bowing in one direction and then another before returning to center stage, where she stood motionless while she waited for the noise to die down.

When it finally did, she still stood motionless. Completely silent. Tate found himself holding his breath.

After long moments, the woman raised both her arms above her head, stretching luxuriantly. Ever so slowly, she lowered one arm, slid her fingers around the back of her neck, then simultaneously jerked her head and moved her hand, flinging out her hair in wild abandonment.

It was the most sensuous gesture Tate had ever seen in his life. He released the breath he'd been holding with a long whoosh.

But Gloria La Grande wasn't finished yet. Not with her performance. And not with him.

She raised her arm again, dramatically holding it over her head for a long moment, then abruptly dropped it and pointed her finger directly at Tate.

"I've got *you*, babe!" she shouted.

The audience whooped and hollered.

Tate blinked again.

"Oh, yes," Gloria whispered directly into the microphone. "'I've got you, babe...'"

It took Tate a moment longer to realize that the singer wasn't talking to him; she was *singing* to him, singing the song Cher had made famous. And never taking her eyes off him while she sang it.

He felt a sudden rush of heat in his cheeks. Damn it all! He couldn't be blushing, could he? No way, he decided. It must be that terrible rotgut he'd been drinking that was making him so warm. And he was slightly giddy, too.

Of course it was the whiskey.

Still... The sexiest woman he'd ever seen in his life was singing directly to him. Him alone.

At least, it seemed that way to Tate. And the other customers must have thought so, too, because they kept looking in his direction.

He was supposed to be here anonymously, drowning his sorrows in private. What if someone he knew happened to see him? But wait. There was no way he'd run into someone he knew; nobody he knew ever ventured into this section of Atlanta.

So go with the flow, he told himself. *Enjoy it. Savor the idea of the sexiest woman you've ever seen, coming on to you like gangbusters.*

She was only doing it to excite the audience, of course. To arouse them to fever pitch. Tate knew that, even in his muzzied state. And he also knew it was working. Almost everybody in the place was standing up now, clapping and singing along with Gloria La Grande.

Tate got up, too, sliding off his stool and immediately wishing he hadn't moved so quickly. He clutched the edge of the counter for support and waited for the room to stop spinning. After a moment, it did.

When Gloria finally finished her song, the place went wild, with everybody yelling and whistling and stomping their feet at the same time. Tate grinned, applauding enthusiastically.

He kept on grinning while Gloria flipped off the switch to the microphone and climbed down from the stage. His grin slipped a little when she started making her way through the crowd, moving in his direction, looking directly at him.

But surely she wouldn't be coming over to him. Would she?

Tate glanced around. His coat occupied one of the bar stools beside his. The other stool was empty.

Would she?

It sure seemed like she would.

She did.

She walked confidently through the throng of people, who stepped aside to make way for her, and sashayed right up to him, only stopping when mere inches separated their bodies. Tate swallowed.

She looked up at him and smiled. Her eyes were blue. Tate was tongue-tied.

"Hi," she said in that arousingly throaty voice of hers.

Tate could only nod.

"Well," she said, still smiling, "are you going to ask me to sit down and have a drink with you, or what?"

Tate finally found his voice. "Sure." It sounded like a croak when it came out. He cleared his throat and pulled out the vacant stool next to him. "What would you like?"

"What are you having?" she asked, arranging her rounded little rear end on the seat.

Tate swallowed again. "Bourbon. But I wouldn't recommend it."

"It's that bad?"

"Worse."

She nodded seriously. "In that case, I'll have a beer."

Tate motioned to the bartender and ordered their drinks.

"What's your name?" Gloria La Grande asked, training her deep blue eyes directly on him.

For a horrifying moment, he couldn't recall it. "Tate Rabun," he finally blurted out.

"Do you live around here?"

He shook his head. "No."

"Where?"

"What?"

"If you don't live around here," she explained with a touch of impatience, "then where *do* you live?"

"Up north," he replied.

"Really?" Gloria La Grande said. "Nashville? New York?"

Tate shook his head again. "North Georgia."

Gloria raised her eyebrows and looked at him for a long moment. Then she threw back her head and laughed. "Score one for you," she said. "You had me going for a while there."

Tate hadn't deliberately set out to mislead her. He'd merely been evasive about where he lived because of some fuzzy-headed notion that he shouldn't reveal too much about himself in case someone was listening. But if she thought he'd done it to amuse her—as it seemed to have done—he certainly wasn't going to tell her otherwise.

The bartender brought their drinks and helped himself to more bills from the rapidly dwindling stack on the counter. Tate saw Gloria glance from the money to him, then back to the bartender. For a moment he thought she was going to say something, but then she seemed to change her mind and took a swallow of her beer instead.

When she arched her head back, Tate saw the smooth whiteness of her throat. He wondered if her skin would be soft and warm under the touch of his fingers.

When her full lower lip touched the rim of her glass, he wondered how her mouth would feel under his. He looked away.

When he turned back to her, she was watching him, her intelligent eyes seeming to see right through him. He knew he was out of his depth here, not only because he'd been drinking but also because he'd never met a woman quite like her before.

"So tell me, Tate Rabun. What did you think of my act?"

"I thought it was great!"

"Really?" she said, sounding pleased.

"Yes. You were wonderful," he added, wanting to please her some more.

"Well. Coming from you, that's quite a compliment."

Tate blinked in confusion. "Coming from me?" he repeated.

"You know... with all the singers you must hear... good and bad." She leaned closer and rested her hand on top of his. "I'm glad you thought I was one of the good ones," she added, giving his hand a little squeeze.

"You are," he stated emphatically. "You're one of the best, Gloria."

She kept her hand on his and leaned even closer. "I'll tell you a secret. Okay?" she whispered. Her warm breath caressed his cheek and sent a shiver up his spine. "Gloria La Grande isn't my real name. It's just a stage name I use. I'm really Maggie Bennett."

Tate wasn't surprised, but wondered whether he should pretend to be.

Maggie leaned away from him. "But you already guessed that, didn't you?"

"Well...Gloria La Grande does sound kind of phony."

"Kind of?"

"Very phony." They both laughed. "Tell me something else, Maggie," he said. "How did you come to...uh...sing at the Green Lantern?"

"At a joint like this, you mean?"

"No!" It was what he'd meant, but he didn't want to hurt her feelings. "I didn't say that. Don't forget that I'm a customer at the Green Lantern."

"But you don't really belong here. You merely came on business."

"Huh?" What was she talking about?

"As a matter of fact, I don't belong here, either." She took a deep draft of her beer. "I had a booking at a big hotel in Cancun, Mexico, one of the plushest hotels in town. But I'm sure you read about what happened."

Tate rubbed his hand across his eyes. "I, uh...I'm not sure. Refresh my memory."

"The hurricane! Remember?"

Tate seemed to recall reading something about a hurricane in Mexico. "I think so."

"Luckily, the guests were able to evacuate in time. But it destroyed almost the entire building. No telling when it will be able to reopen."

"So that left you without a job. I'm sorry."

"Oh, don't feel sorry for me! I have another booking. In Atlantic City. At one of the big casinos."

"You do?" Tate said, impressed.

"You needn't look so surprised. I can do other things besides country and western, you know."

"I didn't mean to..."

"As a matter of fact," Maggie said, gesturing to her clingy black dress, "I do a great Liza. And you should hear my Cole Porter songs." She paused for a moment, then continued in a low, whispery voice, "Care to sample my wares?"

Tate suddenly wished he hadn't had quite so much to drink tonight. He was sure—almost—that Gloria/Maggie was coming on to him. But it was the strangest come-on he'd ever experienced. Maybe that was the way people in show business operated, though.

Maggie smiled at him. Tate smiled back and took a sip of water.

"So, Tate," she said. "Do you think we might be able to work something out between us?"

He choked on his water.

"ARE YOU all right now?" Maggie asked after Tate's coughing had subsided. He nodded, evidently not trusting himself to speak quite yet. She was amazed that one little sip of water had brought on such a violent spasm. It must have gone down the wrong way.

Waiting for him to recover completely, Maggie studied the man beside her. He was big, blond and handsome. And a record producer, to boot. All her romantic fantasies rolled into one. He looked like Nick Nolte's younger brother...if Nick Nolte even had a younger brother.

Somehow, though, he didn't fit her image of a record producer. And when she'd made that reference to sampling her wares, the strangest look had appeared on his face. He obviously didn't have the foggiest notion she was paraphrasing a line from Cole Porter's "Love for Sale." Of course that could be easily explained; he probably specialized in country and western.

Tate finally sighed. "I'm better now."

"I'm glad," Maggie said, giving him another smile. He didn't smile back this time.

"I think I may have had too much to drink tonight," he said slowly, as if he were measuring his words.

Maggie didn't know how to reply to that, so she shrugged.

"What was it you were saying before...about the two of us working something out?"

"Well, you did say you liked my act."

"And you think that means I want to..." Tate stopped, thought for a moment, then started over. "I want to be sure I have this straight. Any arrangement between the two of us...I mean...would it involve money?"

"Of course. You surely wouldn't expect me to work for free, would you?"

"*Work?* Is that what you consider it?"

"Well, I admit I like it—love it—but I have to pay the rent."

"At least you're honest about it," Tate said. "And I'll be honest with you. I've never paid for—uh...this sort of thing in my life. And I have no intention of doing so now."

What a cheapskate! And to think, she'd actually been attracted to him! Maggie shook her head. "With that kind of attitude, I don't see how you get anybody to work for you."

"Believe it or not, it hasn't been a problem. Some women actually seem to find me attractive."

"You scum!"

"What?"

"Using women that way! I suppose you use your so-called charms to cheat them out of royalties later on, too."

"Royalties?" Tate asked.

"It's been so long since you paid them, you've forgotten the word, huh? That doesn't surprise me."

"What the hell are you talking about?"

"I'm talking about *you,* hotshot! You're not only a disgrace to the recording profession, you're a disgrace to the human race!"

Tate shook his head. "I don't see what the recording profession has to do with this."

"Let me spell it out for you, then. You're a record producer and the way you conduct your personal life reflects directly on the entire industry."

He continued shaking his head. "I'm not a record producer."

"You ought to be ashamed of—" Maggie stopped, blinked. "What did you say?"

"I'm not a record producer."

"You're not?"

"No."

"If not . . . then who . . . or what . . . *are* you?"

"I'm a farmer."

"A farmer," Maggie repeated, thoughts spinning wildly, crazily around in her head. "A farmer," she said again, as an outrageous pattern—a regular comedy of errors—began to emerge.

"I thought you were a record producer," she said. "I thought—hoped—the two of us might be able to work out a recording contract." She waited a moment for her words to sink in and saw Tate's gray eyes crinkle at the corners when they did.

Then she recalled the rest of their conversation. "And you thought I . . ." She left the sentence unfinished.

Tate snickered. "I sure did."

Maggie grimaced. "Oh, dear Lord."

They broke into laughter at the same time, and couldn't seem to stop.

What a fiasco, Maggie thought . . . with her assuming he was a record producer and him believing she was a hooker negotiating payment. Thank goodness Tate found the situation amusing. A lot of men wouldn't. And even if he wasn't in the music business, he was still one of the most attractive men she'd ever met.

"That was the best laugh I've had in years," Maggie said finally, wiping tears from her eyes. "A real hoot."

"Sure was," Tate agreed. "Even made me forget my troubles for a while."

"You have troubles, Tate?" Maggie said, sobering. "I'm sorry."

He shrugged.

She reached out her hand and touched his, trying to tell him with her touch that she was on his side. "I'm a good listener, if you want to talk about it."

"Thanks. But I wouldn't know where to begin."

"That bad?"

"Worse. I—"

"Gloria," a man's voice boomed from behind her.

Taking a deep breath, Maggie patted Tate's hand before swiveling around to face the intruder. The man was big and burly, with a ruddy face. He reeked of sweat and alcohol.

"I got to tell you, honey," he said. "That was some kind of show you put on tonight."

She forced a smile. "Thank you."

"Yep," the man repeated. "Some kind of show."

She kept the false smile but didn't speak, hoping the man would go away.

He didn't.

"Wanna dance?" he asked.

Maggie hid her revulsion. "No, thanks."

"Why not?"

Recognizing potential trouble, Maggie tried to diffuse it. "I'm all tuckered out after that show I just did. Maybe another time," she said. *Like in a hundred years.*

The man still didn't go away. His bloodshot gaze moved from her to Tate and back to her again. "What about *him?*" the man asked, gesturing his head in Tate's direction.

"What about him?" Maggie asked ingenuously.

"You don't seem too tired for his company. I saw the two of you holdin' hands and makin' eyes at each other."

This was getting out of hand, Maggie realized. The man was mean, half-drunk and dangerous. "He's my boyfriend," she blurted out, saying the first thing that came to her mind.

"That a fact?" the man said.

She knew she'd made a mistake—a big mistake—even before the brute narrowed his eyes and leered at her. At least she had one thing on her side, she thought nervously. The Green Lantern was packed tonight, and surely the man wouldn't get too rough with so many other people around to watch.

She was wrong.

"Maybe it's time you got yourself a new boyfriend," he said, leaning threateningly closer.

His fetid breath made her sick to her stomach. Or maybe it was her own fear making her ill.

Suddenly, the man reached out a beefy hand and grabbed her wrist, pulling her to her feet. "No!" she protested.

"Let go of her," Tate said, getting off his stool.

"So your fancy boyfriend can speak, after all," the man said with a sneer. "What was that you said, pretty boy?"

"I said let her go," Tate repeated in a low, steely voice. "You bastard."

Chapter Two

That last remark had done the trick, Tate noted with satisfaction. The man released his grip on Maggie and turned his total attention to him instead. *Good.*

"What did you call me?" the ugly brute asked.

"I think you heard me loud and clear," Tate replied, his calm voice belying his mounting excitement. "But just in case you didn't, I'll repeat it for you."

"Nobody calls me that and gets away with it!" the man roared.

"You could leave now and pretend you didn't hear it," Tate suggested, hoping the man wouldn't. Still smarting from his family's betrayal, he needed the release of a good fight.

"You, you…" the man said, growing redder in the face by the moment, his temper clearly about to explode.

"What's the matter?" Tate taunted. "You too scared to speak anymore?"

"Damn you!" The man lifted his big, beefy arm back behind his head, then swung at Tate with all his might.

Tate heard the whoosh of air above his head as he easily ducked the blow. He grinned. "Missed me by a mile."

"Stop it, you two!" Maggie shouted. "Stop it right now!"

"Wanna try again?" Tate challenged. "Wanna look like more of an idiot than you already do?" He was delighted when he saw the man clench his teeth and lower his head, getting ready to charge him.

The man came forward, head down to ram him. Tate sidestepped, remembering at the last moment to put out his foot as the man went past. The man fell with a mighty thud, sprawling on the floor.

"That's enough, Tate," Maggie said, clutching his arm.

He shook off her hand. "The fun's just starting."

"Tate..." she began, then stopped and stared at something—someone—behind him.

Tate turned and saw the giant getting to his feet, murder in his eyes. "Back off, Maggie," Tate said. "This is the real thing."

"But—"

"*Now!*" he commanded. He felt rather than saw her move away from him. He crouched and waited for the man to come at him, knowing the brute was wiser now... and a helluva lot more dangerous.

The fight began in earnest.

They traded blows—a glancing right to Tate's shoulder and a short left to the man's ample belly. Then they grappled, each struggling for the advantage and a chance to land a solid hit. The man made a pretty good jab at Tate's right eye. He felt a warm wetness gliding down his cheek, and knew it was his own blood.

Tate feigned left, then quickly moved right, catching the man off guard with his right fist to send him reeling, then sprawling on the floor again. He took a deep breath. His hand hurt like hell but he suddenly felt alive, felt *good*. Better than he'd felt in days. Weeks, even. This was just what he'd needed to relieve all his frustrations.

Tate crouched, waiting for his opponent to get to his feet again. When he did, Tate hit him with his left fist, then his right. A blow to the cheek, a jab to the eye to pay the man back for the one he'd landed on Tate. Then a solid punch to the belly, followed by an uppercut under the chin. When the man hit the floor this time, Tate felt the heady joy of victory.

He looked around for Maggie and found her still standing beside the bar. He walked over to her, grinning. Maybe she'd kiss him with those lush red lips of hers, just to show her thanks.

She glared at him.

"Why are you looking at me like that?" Tate asked, his grin fading in the face of her obvious disapproval.

"Take one guess."

"I thought you'd thank me for standing up for you."

"*Thank you!* Thank you? You could have been maimed for life. You could have even gotten yourself killed! And I'm supposed to *thank* you?"

"I did it for you," he protested. Fuzzy-headed as he was, he knew that wasn't exactly true. He'd done it as much for himself as for her. He swiped away at the blood flowing from the cut above his eye.

She snorted. "You did it for yourself. Not me."

How did she know that?

Maggie was glaring directly at him, trying to make him feel guilty, Tate knew. But then he saw her eyes shift, and suddenly she was looking at something behind him. "Brace yourself," she said in a low, urgent voice. "It's not over yet."

"I can't believe that guy could get up again," Tate said.

"Not him. His friends."

Tate wheeled around. He swallowed. There were four of them, each bigger than the last one.

He felt Maggie clutch his arm, her fingers digging in. "Let's get out of here," she whispered.

Tate shook his head, knowing he was making the wrong decision but somehow unable to do otherwise.

"There are too many of them," Maggie pleaded urgently. "Don't be stupid."

"I guess I was born stupid," Tate said. "Just a stupid hillbilly."

Taking a deep breath, he stood perfectly still, waiting for the friends of his fallen victim to arrive. The man in front, evidently the leader of the pack, was taller than Tate's first opponent had been. Also leaner. And meaner, he guessed. Mr. Macho himself.

"Haul Bobby Joe off to the side and take care of him, Floyd," Mr. Macho said, keeping his gaze trained on Tate and not even bothering to glance at his friend on the floor. One of the men behind him moved to obey the leader's command.

"You shouldn't have done that to Bobby Joe," Macho said to Tate.

Tate swallowed. "Was that his name?"

"'Cause now we're gonna have to do something about you," the man said.

In spite of his apprehension, Tate felt a sudden surge of adrenaline. Excitement. "A man has to do what he has to do."

"Can't you do something to stop this?" Tate heard Maggie shout from behind him.

"Listen, boys..." the bartender began.

"You stay out of this," one of Macho's cohorts said, pointing his finger directly at the bartender.

"We're going to mop up this place with your sorry face," Macho said to Tate.

The man loved the sound of his own voice, Tate decided, feeling a fleeting desire for the two of them to go at it one on one. He'd like to see just how much of Macho was bluster and how much was the real thing. Obviously, that wasn't going to happen. The other thugs were already moving into place beside their leader. If only he could think of a way...

Tate forced a grin. "You can try, but personally I like the odds. Only four against one."

Bingo.

"Don't kid yourself!" Macho shouted. "I can handle you on my lonesome. Stay out of this, guys," he added, turning to his friends.

"But—" one of the other men protested.

"You heard me!"

Tate crouched, waiting for the onslaught. It came.

Macho came on with a rush, landing a solid blow to Tate's midsection that knocked the air right out of him. Then, while Tate was doubled over with pain, he felt a jackhammer hit his chin, knocking his head back up and sending him sprawling to the floor.

Tate blinked his eyes, trying to clear his vision. He felt as if he'd just been run over by a tank. Had the man really done all this damage with only two punches? And did he really want to hang around for more punishment—having a guy beat his brains out? Maybe he should just roll over and play dead.

No. He'd had too much to drink tonight—way too much—and that had slowed his reflexes, clouded his judgment. But he wasn't a quitter, never had been. And he sure as hell wasn't going to start now. He rolled over onto his side, then gradually climbed to his knees, shaking his head to clear the cobwebs.

"Had enough, pretty boy?"

Tate lifted his head and saw Macho standing right beside him, towering over him, looking about twenty feet tall. Tate shook his head.

Macho laughed and kicked him in the gut.

Tate felt searing pain shoot through him, taking all the breath out of him, and closed his eyes. Opening them again, he saw the man's boot being drawn back to kick him again.

No! He lunged and grabbed the man's ankle before he could follow through with the kick.

Tate was flat on the floor on his stomach now, and knew he was helpless. His mind told him that his only chance to survive this thing was to hold on to the booted foot he was clutching desperately. Macho made an effort to yank his foot free. Tate responded by twisting it sharply to the left.

He heard the man cry out with pain. Then he heard—and felt—Macho fall to the floor with a mighty thud.

Tate forgot his pain in the sudden exhilaration that surged through his entire body. He climbed to his knees again and crawled forward until he was able to grab the man's hair in his hand. He drew back his other hand.

Before Tate could deliver the blow, he felt someone grab his arm, hauling him off Macho and sending him across the floor. *Damn.* One of the other thugs was getting into the act now, and the rest of them would probably follow.

Tate gritted his teeth, determined to at least let them know they'd been in a fight. A helluva fight, he thought, getting to his feet and charging straight at his attackers.

He knocked one of them down by ramming his head into the man's stomach. He sent another one reeling with a fist to the face. The third one picked up a bar stool and threw it at Tate. He ducked, and heard the stool crash into the neatly stacked bottles behind the bar.

Not bad, he thought after the first onslaught. But he knew it was only a matter of time before they'd nail him. After all, they were four against one. *Make that five against one,* he corrected, seeing Bobby Joe on his feet again and coming toward him, madder than ever.

But then, something strange happened. While Tate was grappling with one of Macho's unsavory crew, he gradually became aware that *he* wasn't alone, either. Other people had jumped into the fracas.

Out of the corner of his eye, he saw one of Maggie's accompanists scuffling with Macho. And he spied another man he'd never seen before trading blows with one of Macho's thugs. Two complete strangers, neither of whom he'd ever seen before, were going at each other.

A simple fight was turning into an all-out brawl.

He grinned, his adrenaline surging again as he shook off his current opponent, then landed a blow that sent the man to the floor. He looked around to see who would challenge him next.

Tate's grin abruptly faded—disappeared—when he saw that Maggie had joined in the free-for-all. She had jumped onto Bobby Joe's back. Her legs were wound around the burly man's middle and she was pummeling him wildly with her fists.

"Maggie! Dammit!" Tate shouted, pushing faceless, sweaty bodies aside as he headed in her direction, intent on rescuing her. He'd almost reached her when he felt someone's hand on his shoulder, whirling him around with brute force.

Tate never saw the man's face. A fist came toward him and he heard the sickening sound of bone crushing bone. He felt a searing, white-hot pain in the cheek beneath his right eye.

A woman screamed. Maggie?

The whole world went dark as he fell off the edge of it.

WATER.

Tate tried to swallow, but his mouth was so dry he couldn't. He'd give everything he owned for a sip of water right now. A mere teaspoon.

He opened his eyes. *Correction.* His eye. The left one. Something seemed to have happened to his right one.

Then, gradually, he recalled what that something was. He groaned.

"Tate?"

Out of a fog, he saw her face take shape in front of him. An anxious face. Maggie. He was lying on hard, cold asphalt and she was leaning over him.

"Are you awake now?" she asked.

"No," he mumbled. His voice was thick and croaky.

"I was starting to get really worried about you," Maggie said, gently touching a damp cloth to his cheek. "You were out for so long."

"That cloth smells funny," Tate said, wrinkling his nose with distaste.

"I wet your handkerchief with beer."

"Beer?"

"It was the only liquid I could find out here in the parking lot," she said defensively. "But don't worry. The can hadn't been opened when I found it, so it's clean beer."

Tate tried to laugh, but it came out sounding more like a groan.

"Aren't you going to ask the usual questions?" Maggie said.

"What questions?"

"Like, 'What happened? Where am I?' You know, like they do in the movies."

"Unfortunately, I remember what happened. And you just told me we're in the parking lot. How'd we get here?"

"Ted and Robbie helped me drag you out after... uh... you got knocked down."

"Ted and Robbie?"

"My accompanists," she replied impatiently, as if he should know that.

Tate shifted his head to glance around. The slight movement hurt. "Where are they now?"

"They left after we got you safely out here. And that was after the manager fired all three of us and threatened to call the cops if we ever showed our faces at the Green Lantern again."

"Oh, hell." Tate slowly and painfully raised himself to a sitting position. "I'm sorry."

Maggie shrugged.

"Thanks for staying with me, though," he said. "Taking care of me and all."

"You're welcome." Maggie leaned back on her knees and looked at him for a long moment. "I figured it was the least I could do."

Tate managed a grin. "I thought you blamed me for the whole thing."

"I decided it wasn't *entirely* your fault. You had some help."

"And speaking of help," he said, his grin widening, "I saw you tangling with ole Bobby Joe back in there. Did you do any damage?"

"I managed to get in a few licks. Drew blood," she added with a certain amount of pride.

"With your fists?" Tate said with surprise, remembering the awkward way she'd been pummeling Bobby Joe.

"Fingernails."

Tate laughed and after a moment, Maggie joined him.

"Well," he said finally, "I guess I've had enough excitement for one night. I'd better be getting home."

Maggie helped him struggle to his feet. The parking lot started spinning, and Tate clutched Maggie's shoulder for support. "You don't look so hot," she said.

"I'll be okay in a minute," he insisted, although he wasn't at all sure of that. He might never be okay again.

His dizziness got a little better finally and he looked around for his car. "There it is," he said with relief when he spotted it at last.

"What?"

"My car."

"Oh," Maggie said. "Would you help me hail a taxi, so I can get to my apartment?"

"Well . . . sure." It was the least he could do, considering how she'd stayed around to watch out for him. Then he frowned. "How'd you get out here earlier tonight?" The Green Lantern Grille and Tavern was in the boonies, at the edge of nowhere.

"I came with Ted and Robbie."

"And they just went off and left you stranded?"

"I insisted they leave," Maggie replied huffily. "There was a chance that the manager would change his mind and call the police, after all, and I didn't want them to be here if the cops came. They're both . . . uh . . . on parole."

"On parole?" Tate repeated. "From prison?"

"No, from Sunday school," Maggie said. "Of course from prison. And don't look so holier-than-thou. You could have wound up in jail tonight yourself if we hadn't helped you out. It's a misdemeanor to destroy private property, not to mention the battery case Bobby Joe could have made against you."

Tate swallowed. He'd never thought of that. "I'm sorry," he whispered. Then he thought of something. If both Robbie and Ted had prison records, did that mean that Maggie, too, might be...

"Don't say it," she suddenly warned. "Don't even think it. My record's clean. I've never been caught...so far."

Were his thoughts that transparent? Tate wondered. And what had Maggie meant by *so far?* He cleared his throat. "Forget the taxi, I'll drive you home."

"Wait a second while I get your jacket."

"My jacket! You can't go back inside..."

She laughed. "It's not inside the tavern. I draped it on the hood of a Chevy close to where you were lying." Maggie moved away but was back in a second, holding his suit jacket in her hand.

"How on earth did you happen to think of bringing the jacket in the first place?" Tate marveled. "And why?"

"I saw a guy headed out the door with it and grabbed it from him. It looked like a nice jacket. Expensive. I thought you wouldn't want to lose it."

Tate could only shake his head in wonder. "Thanks again."

They started walking toward his car, but he had to stop every few steps because everything started spinning again.

Maggie finally stopped and shook her head. "It could be all that whiskey you drank tonight...or a concussion from the fight. Or both. Whatever, you're really in no shape to drive.''

"I'll feel better after a while," he said, inhaling a deep breath of the fresh night air.

"No."

Tate was forced to agree with her. He was in such wobbly shape, he wouldn't even want to ride with himself driving. "Maybe you could..." he began, looking at Maggie.

"I could," she said. "If you don't mind riding with someone driving without a license."

"You don't have a driver's license?"

"I didn't bring it with me tonight."

Tate rubbed his hand across his eyes, trying to think. "We'll both take a taxi and I can come back to get my car when I feel better."

Maggie nodded her approval. They turned around and headed toward the Green Lantern, where miraculously a taxi was waiting in front of the entrance. "Hold up for a second," Maggie said, clutching Tate's arm. "You need to put on your jacket before we get there."

"Why?"

"Because there's blood all over your shirt. I doubt that a driver would even let us into his cab in the condition you're in."

Looking down at himself, Tate saw that what she said was true. He struggled into the jacket, feeling a new pain or pang with each movement he made. When he finally had the jacket on, he straightened his tie and combed his fingers through his hair.

"That's better. And remember to keep the right side of your face turned away from the driver as much as possible," Maggie said. "How do I look?"

Tate looked at her and grinned. "Beautiful."

She rolled her eyes. "You want us both to have to *walk* home?"

He blinked his good eye to clear his vision, then studied her more closely. "There's a smear on your cheek. Do you still have that handkerchief you soaked in beer?"

She handed it to him. "It's mostly covered with blood."

Tate examined the handkerchief and finally found a clean corner. He rubbed it against her cheek gently, then peered at her again. Traces of the smear were still there, so Tate touched the handkerchief with the tip of his tongue to moisten it before rubbing her cheek again.

Maggie's eyes widened with surprise.

"My mother used to do this to me," he explained. "It's not exactly hygienic, but it works."

Maggie didn't say anything. Her expression was unreadable.

"There!" Tate said when he'd finished. "That should do the trick."

"It better," Maggie said ominously.

Tate stood up as straight as he could and tried to appear confident as they approached the taxi. The driver, lounging against the front fender and smoking a cigarette, grinned and tossed the butt aside when they walked up to him. "Where to, folks?" he asked pleasantly.

Tate looked at Maggie; she gave the cabbie her address. The driver opened the back door. "Nice night," he commented as Maggie and Tate climbed inside the cab.

"Yeah," Tate muttered. "He didn't even give us a second glance," he whispered to Maggie after the driver closed the door and headed around the car to his own seat in front. "You'd think people came out of the Green Lantern looking like war casualties every night."

Maggie giggled. "Maybe they do."

Tate smiled. He took a deep breath and relaxed a little, feeling secure in the darkness, feeling the warmth of Maggie seated right beside him.

He took another deep breath and relaxed some more, sliding a little closer to Maggie until their hips and thighs were touching. He felt the heat of her through his trousers and through the little black dress she wore. He sighed and leaned his head back against the seat.

"This is nice," he whispered, feeling warm and alive.

"A smelly taxi is nice?" she whispered back, her breath fluttering against his cheek and causing him to feel even warmer and more alive.

"Being here safe with you makes it nice."

"Now that was a nice thing to say."

"I can think of something that would be even nicer," he said, turning his head to look at her. Her head was resting against the back of the seat, too, and she was watching him, her face only inches from his.

"What?"

"I had it in mind to kiss you."

"Wouldn't that be painful for you?"

"Nobody hit me in the mouth. At least, not that I remember."

"Mmm. Well, it's a fact that I've never kissed a farmer before."

"Then it's about time you did," Tate said. Tilting his head, he closed the distance between them and touched his lips to hers. Her mouth was warm, soft and responsive, exactly as he'd imagined it would be. A man could happily spend a lifetime exploring a mouth like hers.

Tate shifted in his seat, draping his arm around her narrow shoulders to pull her closer. Then, increasing the pressure of his lips on hers until they parted, he thrust his tongue inside, exploring the sweet, moist interior. After long moments, she pulled away.

"Do all farmers kiss like that?" she asked softly.

"I don't know. I've never kissed one." He thought for a moment. "Does that mean you liked it, or you didn't?"

"Did. Definitely."

"I'm glad," he said, kissing her cheek before sliding his mouth lower to nibble her neck. The movement caused a sharp pain in his ribs and a groan escaped before he could stifle it.

"You've hurt yourself!" she said.

"It was worth it. Every bit of it," he said, lifting his head.

Maggie leaned back, her arms resting on his shoulders as she gazed at him. "Crazy man," she whispered.

"Yes," he whispered back. "Did you ever kiss a crazy man before?"

"Never."

"Looks like tonight's your lucky night. First you got to kiss a farmer and now a crazy man."

Maggie moved her mouth to his and tightened her arms around his neck. "Lucky me," she murmured against his lips.

They kissed forever. Or a reasonable facsimile.

"Here we are, folks," the taxi driver said. "This is the address you gave me."

Maggie lifted her head and blinked her eyes, looking as dazed as Taté felt. "When did we stop moving?" she asked.

"I don't think the two of us *have* stopped moving," Tate said. "But the taxi has. Is this the right place?"

Maggie pushed her hair back in a totally seductive, totally feminine gesture and leaned over to peer out the window. "It looks like it," she said, a note of regret in her voice.

Tate thought he knew the reason for her regret. And also thought he might have a remedy for it. Why didn't he just stay here—with Maggie—for tonight? With that happy thought, he released his hold on her and allowed her to scramble out the door of the cab.

"Do you have your key?" he said, painfully climbing out of the cab to join her on the sidewalk.

"Of course," she said, smiling as she tugged at a small silver chain around her neck and pulled up her house key from its resting place between her breasts. She took the key from the chain and held it up proudly.

Tate sighed with relief. "Listen, there's something I'd like to—"

"Hey! I can't hang around here all night," the cabbie shouted.

"Just a minute," Tate shouted back, holding up his hand.

"You were saying?" Maggie said.

"I was going to ask if I could..."

"You wanna go someplace else, or pay me now and stay here?" the driver shouted, getting out of the car.

"That's what I was going to ask," Tate blurted out. "If I could come in for a minute."

"I don't know, Tate..."

"Just for a little while," he said, lying through his teeth. "A drink of water."

"Make up your mind!" the cabbie said, on the sidewalk beside them now.

"That's all?" Maggie asked Tate.

"I'd almost sell my soul for a drink of water," he said, remembering how thirsty he'd been earlier.

"Well..." Maggie said hesitantly.

"Hey you. I'm talking to you," the cabbie said.

"I can call another taxi later on," Tate said, trying to look thirsty. "Please?"

"I guess," she said with a shrug. "But only for a drink of water," she added, narrowing her eyes.

"Then I'll be out of here," Tate said, giving her what he hoped was an innocent smile. Maggie headed for her front door and Tate turned to the taxi driver, grinning with satisfaction. "How much do I owe you?"

"Fourteen dollars, seventy-five cents."

"A bargain," Tate said, reaching into his back pocket for his money.

It wasn't there.

He reached in his other back pocket.

It was empty, too.

Tate started searching all his pockets, growing more frantic by the moment.

"Whassa matter?" the taxi driver asked suspiciously.

"I seem to have...uh...lost my money, somehow. I can't find it."

"I can accept plastic," the man said.

"That's another problem," Tate said, attempting a smile. "All my credit cards are missing, too."

Maggie screamed.

Tate wheeled around to look at her. "Maggie?"

"My key doesn't fit the door!" she shouted. "I've been locked out of my own apartment!"

Tate heard a strangled sound coming from the cab driver and turned back to face him, just in time to see the man draw back his fist to hit him.

Oh, hell, Tate thought as he saw the man's fist headed his way. *Here we go again.*

Instinctively, Tate threw up his arms to protect himself and took a step backward. The driver's blow didn't do any further damage to his battered face, but somehow Tate's feet got tangled up and he went sprawling on his rear end anyway.

"You brute!" Maggie screeched, running toward the taxi driver with both arms raised to attack.

"That does it!" the man said, retreating toward his car. "I'm calling the cops!"

"Did he hurt you?" Maggie asked, leaning over Tate with an anxious expression.

"Only my...ego," Tate said, rubbing his rear end as he got to his feet again. "But we need to get out of here in a hurry." He gestured to the cab, where the driver was already talking on his two-way radio.

"Which way?" Maggie asked.

They both heard the siren in the distance at the same time. "That way," Tate said, pointing in the opposite direction. He grabbed her hand and they started running.

"Those cops," Maggie said after a few moments. "They couldn't be after us this fast, could they?"

"Hey! You two!"

Tate turned his head and saw the cabbie racing down the sidewalk behind them. "Stop where you are!" the driver shouted. "Right now!"

"I dunno," Tate said to Maggie. "But I'd rather not wait around to find out."

They continued running. Each step Tate took on the pavement set off a new round of pain that shot through his entire body. He didn't think he could go much farther. Looking behind them, Tate saw the driver still in hot pursuit. For such a short guy, the man was amazingly fast.

And the sirens seemed to be getting closer.

Run, Tate, run. Run, Maggie, run.

Tate was gasping for breath. And then he saw it. Their salvation. Maybe.

It was a pickup truck stopped for a traffic light. And it even had its tailgate down. Too winded to talk, Tate punched Maggie with his finger, then pointed to the truck. She nodded in understanding.

The traffic light changed.

"Hurry," Tate gasped.

With a final burst of speed, they reached the truck just as it started to pull away. In one desperate motion, Tate half lifted, half shoved Maggie onto the truck and threw himself on top of her.

Panting, Tate rolled onto his side and looked out the back of the truck. He saw the irate taxi driver pull up short, stop running and shake his fist in their direction.

Maggie slowly got to her knees, put her fingers to her mouth, and blew the cabbie a farewell kiss.

Chapter Three

"Whew! That was some narrow escape," Maggie said.

Tate looked at her; she looked back at him. They both burst out laughing at the same time.

"I swear, Maggie," Tate said when he was finally able to catch his breath. "I don't think I've laughed so much in my whole life."

He pulled out his handkerchief to wipe the tears from his eyes, and that set Maggie off into new gales of laughter. "What?" he said.

She pointed to the handkerchief.

He looked down and saw, in the fleeting illumination from a streetlight, that it was the same bloodstained one she'd used to clean him up at the Green Lantern.

Tate shook his head and laughed along with her. He crumpled up the handkerchief to throw it away but changed his mind at the last minute and stuffed it back into his pocket. "A souvenir of my wild night on the town," he explained to Maggie when he saw the question in her eyes.

She nodded. "What happens next?"

"We'll jump off as soon as the truck slows down. It's bound to stop for another traffic light sooner or later."

"And?"

"Well, I have a few coins in my pocket." He took a deep breath and expelled it. "I guess I'll have to call someone to come and get me." But that someone sure as hell wouldn't be his brother, Brian.

"And?" Maggie asked in a small voice.

Oh, hell! He'd completely forgotten that Maggie had been locked out of her apartment. "And we'll take you wherever you want to go, of course." He paused. She didn't speak, either.

"Uh...you said they changed the locks on your apartment?"

She nodded. "Because I didn't pay this week's rent on time. I was planning to pay it with the money I made tonight."

She was really living close to the edge, Tate thought, feeling a tightening in his gut. "Maybe you can stay with some friends?"

"The only people I know in Atlanta are Ted and Robbie, my accompanists."

"Great guys!"

"And I only met them yesterday."

Tate thought for a moment, then made a decision. "And you know me," he said quietly.

"Listen, I don't want you to feel responsible for—"

"I don't." He held up both hands. "Truly, I don't. But I know lots of people up at Lake Lanier. They'd be happy to put you up for a few days...or at least until you leave for your job in Atlantic City."

Maggie shook her head. "I don't have a booking in Atlantic City, Tate."

He hesitated. "I figured that, Maggie."

"Or anywhere."

"I guessed that, too."

"And even in spite of the fact that I lied to you..."

"Hell, Maggie! I had the best time with you tonight that I've ever had in my life. We're friends. I owe you one."

He thought for a moment that she was going to cry. But she didn't. She bit her bottom lip instead and after a long moment, she grinned. "I guess you do, at that. And it's about time you paid up."

"Damn right," Tate said, reaching out to put his arm around her shoulders. He hugged her to his side, ignoring the pain in his rib cage.

"But don't think that I won't—"

The truck made a sudden swerve to the right and picked up speed, cutting Maggie off. It was all Tate could do to hold on to her—and on to the side of the truck with his other hand—to prevent them both from being swept away. Keeping a firm grip on Maggie, he tried to gradually inch them both farther back into the truck bed.

"What happened?" Maggie asked.

"I think," Tate said, looking around and assessing their situation, "that you and I don't have to worry about where we'll go and what we'll do for the time being."

"What do you mean?"

"The driver of this vehicle just pulled onto the freeway. Heading west, I think. There's no way we'll be able to get off until he decides to stop. Wherever and whenever that may be."

"So we're trapped here in the back of this truck?"

"Yes... unless you're brave enough to jump out at fifty-plus miles an hour. And I'm not," he added.

She shuddered. "Neither am I."

"Let's crawl up closer to the cab," he said, holding her hand tightly while he guided her along. "It should be more comfortable there." Also, there would be less danger of their accidentally being thrown out of the truck.

"And safer," Maggie said, reading his thoughts.

He nodded.

TATE RABUN WAS the nicest man she'd ever met, Maggie decided, trying to make herself comfortable on the sacks of feed he had arranged for them up close to the cab in the back of the pickup. He'd even insisted that she wear his jacket to ward off the cool night air whizzing around them.

Correction. Make that *cold* night air, she thought, shivering as the truck sped through the darkness.

"Still cold?" Tate asked from his huddled position beside her.

She nodded, too uncomfortable to lie about it.

"Me, too," he admitted. "Let's try a different approach. Take off the jacket and we'll lie down and wrap it over us."

Tate rearranged a couple of feed sacks while Maggie removed his jacket. Then he pulled her down, facing him, and spread his jacket over their shoulders. "Better?" he said.

"Yes," she replied, her teeth still chattering.

"It's still not quite right. Lift your head for a second."

Maggie did as he said and he slid one arm under her. Then, holding the jacket, he put his other arm over her. "There," he said with satisfaction. "We should both be warmer in a few minutes."

Maggie was already warmer, and knew it had nothing to do with being protected from the wind. It was because she was lying in a cozy cocoon in the arms of the most attractive man she'd met in a long, long time. Maybe forever. *But don't forget you're in the back of a pickup truck hurtling through the night headed for God knows where,* she reminded herself.

"Maybe we should try to get some sleep," Tate said.

Sleep? Maggie thought with amazement. *At a time like this?*

"Don't worry," Tate said. "I'm sure I'll wake up as soon as the truck stops moving."

"I'm not sleepy."

"Oh."

"Are you?" she asked.

"Well . . . no. Not really. But I thought you might be."

She shook her head. "No." Tate was silent, and she wondered what he was thinking. *Oh, dear. Maybe he thinks I'm suggesting that we take up where we left off in the taxi, and he's completely turned off the idea.*

"Maybe we could talk," she said quickly. "Until we get sleepy."

"Sure. Good idea."

Silence stretched between them like a yawning chasm.

Say something, Maggie. Anything. "Tell me about your farm," she said.

"Farm?" he repeated.

"Yes." She frowned as a sudden thought occurred to her. "Or were you telling fibs the same way I was?"

"No! I mean, I do have a farm. A chicken farm. But there's not much to tell. It's just a farm. And I raise broilers. You know...young, tender chickens. In coops. That's about all there is to it."

Maggie instinctively sensed that that *wasn't* all there was to it...and that Tate was deliberately evading her question. Should she continue probing, prying into his private affairs? Probably not. It was probably the last thing she should do.

"Tell me, Tate," she said, plowing ahead anyway. "Does the farm have anything to do with your troubles . . . the ones you mentioned earlier tonight?"

She sensed his reluctance, and could almost hear him thinking, *Should I tell her? Or tell her to mind her own business?*

"Did I say something about troubles?" he asked.

He was stalling, of course. "Yes," she stated emphatically. "While we were laughing about the mix-up we had—with me thinking you were a record producer and you thinking I was a hooker—you said it had made you forget your troubles for a while."

"Do you remember everything a person says and hold it against him later?"

"Just about."

"You should have warned me earlier."

"You didn't ask me earlier," she pointed out. "But do your troubles have to do with the farm, Tate?"

"In a way. But there's a lot more to it than that."

"I figured there was."

"It goes a long way back."

She nodded. "Big problems usually do."

"But what it boils down to," Tate said angrily, "is that my younger brother is selling my company down the river. The company *I* created, and worked my butt off to make successful. Not only that, but my mother is supporting Brian all the way."

Maggie frowned. "You lost me there. What kind of company are we talking about? A farming company?"

"A cooperative. The Southern Chicken Farmers Co-op. We call it the SCFC for short."

"I'm still confused," she said. "How does the farm fit into all this?"

"Are you really interested?" He narrowed his eyes. "Or are you just being polite?"

"I'm really interested. Besides—trapped like we are and all—what else is there to do?"

Tate tightened his arms around her and gave a roguish grin. "I can think of a couple of things."

So, he wasn't immune to her after all, Maggie thought with satisfaction. "You said you'd already had enough excitement for one night," she reminded him.

Tate relaxed his arms around her and groaned. "You *do* remember everything."

"I warned you. Now tell me about how the farm fits in with the SCFC."

Tate sighed. "My daddy died during my second year of agriculture school at the University of Georgia. Being the oldest and all, I dropped out of school and took over running the farm.

"I grubbed along for a while, just like he'd done all his life. Then gradually, I started changing things a little, using ideas I'd learned in ag school. Nobody was more surprised than I was when they actually worked. Pretty soon, we were showing a profit...enough to make me want more. So I talked other farmers in the area into joining me and my mother in a co-op—the SCFC—with me as president and chief executive officer. The other farmers became members of the board of directors."

Tate paused, obviously remembering those early years.

"And that's when the trouble started?" Maggie said, prompting him to continue.

"Hell, no! The SCFC was a big success, almost from the word go. By joining together, we had increased purchasing power and were able to buy feed cheaper. I introduced the other farmers to things I'd learned in school—better breeding, better feed, disease control and things like that.

"After the co-op was going, I put Mom in charge as general manager and spent my time acting as broker for the group to get the best prices. I was on the road almost constantly.

"Then I found a processing plant that was closed down. It was going for a song. I tried to talk the SCFC board into buying it, but they wouldn't, so I talked the bank into lending me money to buy it myself and fix it up. I signed an exclusive contract with the co-op, guaranteeing to buy all the broilers they could produce and to pay them the top-going price."

"Wasn't that a tremendous gamble?" Maggie asked.

"Not for the co-op, but it sure as hell was for me." He grinned. "But it paid off. Within a year, the processing plant was on its feet, we had contracts lined up with some of the top grocery chains in the area and everybody was making money hand over fist. 'Course it didn't hurt that about that same time, the government came out with new studies showing how healthy it is to eat chicken."

"A little favorable publicity is always nice," Maggie said with a smile.

"That's for sure."

"But if things were going so well, when did the trouble start?" Tate's smile disappeared. Maggie felt his body grow tense, and saw a muscle working in his cheek.

"About a year ago," he said in a low voice. "When my brother got his master's degree and I made the mistake of taking him into the company. Hell, I was the one who made him a member of the board of directors, so I'm mainly to blame for the whole mess."

"What did he do?"

"He started right in trying to make changes—throwing out all the things that had worked for us for years, and converting to computers. You've never seen such a mess! It took months and months to straighten it out."

"Is, uh . . . is it working now?" Maggie asked.

"Yes. Finally." Tate looked at her. "And I see the point you're making. Brian is making changes the same way I did when I first took over the farm. But I made changes gradually. Brian jumps in with both feet, whole hog, sink or swim. He's too impatient. He doesn't seem to realize you don't have to pull the tooth in order to cure the toothache. There are less drastic ways to treat the problem."

Tate narrowed his eyes. "In case you're wondering, I'm not talking about Brian this way because of jealousy. Even though I've disagreed with him, I've tried to support him. I've given him latitude to try out new ideas . . . maybe too much latitude. Maybe if I'd put my foot down on his latest harebrained scheme, things wouldn't have gone as far as they have, and I wouldn't be on the brink of losing everything I've worked for all these years."

"It's that bad?" Maggie whispered, feeling the tenseness in his body.

"Yes. That bad."

"What happened?"

"Several months ago, Brian took it in his head that we needed to expand the SCFC . . . possibly even go national. I told him to look into possibilities and give me a written report. He did a damn sight more than that."

There was no humor in Tate's brief, harsh laugh. "He contacted some of his fancy MBA friends—fraternity brothers he'd been in school with—and they put him in touch with a so-called 'financial consortium.' That's their phrase, not mine. A bunch of crooked, big-city money-lenders is what I'd call them.

"I'll have to hand it to Brian. He didn't waste time. When I realized how far things had gone, he'd already persuaded most of the SCFC board of directors—including our mother—to agree to merge with the Mid-south Investment Company. They formally voted on it today... yesterday, it is now. All that's left to make it official is my signature on the merger documents.

"I stormed out of the meeting yesterday before they could force me to sign on the spot," he added. "Not that my protest gesture will do any good, except to postpone the inevitable."

Maggie thought about what he'd told her. "What makes you think the consortium is crooked?" she finally asked.

"Mainly a gut feeling. Nothing concrete. I heard a few rumors, but didn't have time to follow up on them because Brian pushed the thing through too fast."

"Couldn't you persuade the board to hold off? At least until you had time to investigate?"

"Believe me, I tried," Tate said wearily. "But with Brian promising the sun and moon and stars, and Mom backing him all the way, the board of directors went crazy. They were seeing dollar signs instead of reason, and I didn't have a chance. I finally said to hell with it and got out of there."

And went to the Green Lantern to drown your sorrows, Maggie thought. In addition to being furious, he must have been terribly hurt that his mother would join forces with his younger brother against him.

Tate had been forced to drop out of school after his father died. But his brother Brian had graduated, even gone on to a master's degree. And who had paid for

Brian's education? Tate, of course. Then his younger brother had repaid his generosity by stabbing him in the back, trying to wrest control of the company and putting the entire works in jeopardy because of his own selfish ambition. And to compound the whole wretched business, Tate's mother had supported his brother's reckless scheme.

Maggie suspected that it wasn't simply losing control, or even losing the company itself, that upset Tate so much. It was the idea of being betrayed by the people he loved most that was tearing him apart.

"So that's all there is?" Maggie said disbelievingly. "You're giving up?"

"What else can I do?" he replied angrily.

"Maybe you could talk to your mother and brother... try to reason with them."

"Reason with those two? Not in this lifetime. The minute I go back, they'll force me to sign those damned merger papers. And then it's all over. I'm trapped between a rock and a hard place."

Maggie tried to think of something else Tate might be able to do, but couldn't come up with anything. "I'm sorry," she said. She heard—and felt—Tate catch his breath.

"What did you say?" he asked in slow, measured tones.

Maggie heard the barely suppressed fury in his voice, and knew she'd made a mistake. But there was no way out of it now. "I said... I'm sorry."

"Sorry for what?"

"Because all those bad things happened to you. Your mother and brother and all—"

"Listen to me, and listen close. I don't want your pity."

"I only meant—"

"Do you understand?" he shouted.

"Yes!" she shouted back. "I understand more than you know." Maggie rolled over, turning her back to him and fuming with righteous indignation. "And to hell with you," she muttered.

TATE LOOKED at the back of Maggie's dark head and silently hurled curses at himself. He was furious because he'd spilled his guts out the way he had. And then, when Maggie had offered her sympathy, he'd lashed out at her. *Damn.*

What had gotten into him? All his life, he'd never been one to complain. If something bothered him, he kept it to himself. If he had a problem, he solved it himself. What had caused him to act differently this time?

Maybe all that whiskey he drank last night had loosened his tongue. Or maybe—just maybe—nothing in his life had ever upset him as much as the situation with his mother and his brother and the SCFC. Even his father's death, traumatic as it was, hadn't caused him to lose control the way this mess had done.

And there was one more possibility. Maybe Maggie had touched a raw nerve when she'd suggested he was giving up without a fight.

He sighed. Whatever the reasons for his unusual behavior, he had no right to take his frustration out on Maggie. He touched her shoulder. She grunted.

"Are you asleep?" he asked.

"No," came the muffled reply.

"I, uh . . . I just want you to know I'm sorry."

She swiveled her head around to look over her shoulder at him. "Sorry for what?" she said, repeating the words he'd used.

He deserved that. "I'm sorry I lashed out at you a little while ago. You were being kind and I shouldn't have done that."

She shrugged.

"Will you forgive me?"

"I guess."

"Thank you."

"You're welcome," she said, suppressing a yawn.

"Do you want to talk some more?"

"I'm a little sleepy now. Maybe we should get some rest."

"That's a good idea," Tate said, although he wasn't the least bit sleepy. He pulled his jacket tighter around her shoulders. "Are you warm enough?"

"Mmm," she said, nestling her back closer to the front of him, spoon-style. "Good night, Tate."

"Good night, Maggie."

As the pickup truck sped along the freeway, Tate felt rather than heard Maggie's breathing. After a short time, its steady rhythm told him she was asleep. He continued holding her close while his mind replayed the events of the past few days, the past few hours. One significant statement of hers kept repeating itself.

"So that's all there is?" she had asked incredulously when he told her about his company's upcoming merger. *"You're giving up?"*

He had angrily responded that there was nothing else he could do. And there wasn't. Was there? *Was there?*

Tate took a deep breath. He'd never been a quitter. Nobody had ever suggested that he was a quitter. Until Maggie.

But wasn't that exactly what he was doing now?

Never mind that he'd barely been able to see past his hurt at his mother's and brother's betrayal. Never mind that the task of proving the financial consortium was crooked seemed impossible. Was he going to just roll over and play dead for the first time in his life?

Was he going to give up without a fight?

"No," he said out loud. An excitement started to build inside him. *"Hell, no!"*

Tate's mind was suddenly clear—focused for the first time since this whole sorry business had begun. He started making plans.

Chapter Four

"Maggie! Wake up!"

Tate shook her shoulder in an attempt to rouse her. "Wake up," he whispered.

Maggie's eyes and mouth opened at the same time. "Wha—" she began.

"The truck's stopped and we need to get out of here," Tate said, pulling her up to a sitting position.

Maggie blinked a couple of times against the brightness of early dawn. "Where are we?" she asked, following his lead by whispering, too.

"At a truck stop. The Midway Truck Stop. I'm not sure where it is, but the driver just went inside and we need to leave before he gets back."

Maggie nodded, scrambled to the edge of the truck bed and agilely jumped to the ground. Tate followed slowly, every muscle in his body creaking and groaning in protest with each move he made. The thunderous pounding in his head had its own staccato rhythm.

"You look like hell," Maggie said in a normal voice when they were safely on the ground away from the truck.

Tate moved his fingers across the stubble on his face and looked down at the dusty, rumpled trousers and bloodstained shirt. "No worse than I feel," he said. "How are you holding up?"

"What do you think?" she asked, holding out both her arms and inviting his appraisal.

He appraised her.

"Not bad," he said, lying. Truth was, she looked sexy as hell with her black hair all tousled around her face the way it was, and with her clear, bright blue eyes. Her clingy black dress was a little dusty but not even wrinkled.

"I could do with a comb," she said. "And a toothbrush."

Tate rummaged through the pockets of his jacket and finally produced a comb. "Sorry, no toothbrush," he said, holding out the comb and belatedly realizing it was so small that it wouldn't be much use to her.

"Thanks," Maggie said, gracefully accepting it without additional comment. "Do you have any idea where the bathrooms are?"

Tate shook his head. "Outside, I hope."

They were. Tate stepped into the well-lit men's room and was relieved to find it clean. He hoped the ladies' room was, too.

Tate stood in front of the mirror behind the lavatory and assessed the damage. "Maggie was right," he said to his reflection. "You do look like hell."

He took off his shirt and was glad to see that only a few small blood stains had penetrated to his undershirt. He threw the dress shirt into the garbage. Then, remembering the bloody handkerchief he'd thought about saving as a souvenir, he took that out of his pocket and threw it into the garbage, too. He removed his undershirt, scrubbed it with cold water and draped it over the counter to dry while he washed his upper torso with soap from the dispenser. After that, he gently blotted himself dry with paper towels, emitting several grunts and groans in the process. Damn, but he was sore!

He finally turned the faucet wide open and ducked his head underneath the spigot, letting the cool, soothing water cascade through his hair and over his face. That felt so good, he was reluctant to get out.

At last he did, toweling his face and hair with some more paper towels, then using damp paper towels to remove the dust from his jacket and trousers. Finally, he picked up his undershirt and examined it. The stains hadn't washed out completely, and the thing was still damp in front. He decided to put it on backward, tucking it into his trousers, then shrugged into his suit jacket. He raked his fingers though his wet hair a couple of times and examined himself in the mirror again.

Not great. But not nearly as bad as before.

Not only that, but he'd found almost three dollars in change in various pockets. That was certainly enough to buy coffee and aspirin out here in the boondocks. Tate straightened his shoulders and went out to meet Maggie.

"I feel almost like a human being again," she said, echoing his thoughts. "And look at you!" she added, her eyes widening. "Except for that black eye and a dark suit instead of white linen, you could be a slightly dissolute southern gentleman."

Tate shook his head. "I'm no gentleman. But I'll treat you to a cup of coffee anyway."

Maggie's eyes widened still more.

"I found some change in my pockets," he explained.

"You're on," she said, looping her arm through his. "Right now, a cup of coffee sounds heavenly."

The truck stop dining room was big, bright and blessedly air-conditioned. Even though it was still early, the temperature outside had turned hot and humid as soon as the sun came up. There were only about a half-dozen customers and plenty of seats. Tate guided Maggie to a booth by the windows and sat down across from her.

"Hi, folks. What can I get you?"

Tate hadn't heard or seen the waitress approach, but there she was beside their booth, big as life. Or maybe a little bigger. She wore a white starched apron stretched across her ample girth, a friendly smile on her ruddy, middle-aged face, and an old-fashioned mesh hair net on her head.

"Hi," Tate said, returning her smile. "We'd like two coffees. And do you have some aspirin?"

The woman gave a hearty guffaw. "We wouldn't be much of a truck stop if we didn't carry the necessities. Back in a sec."

"Do you have any idea where we are?" Maggie asked as soon as the waitress left.

"Sort of. The sign outside said Planters' Junction. As well as I can recall, it's somewhere in South Georgia."

"A long way south?"

Tate nodded.

"How do we get back to Atlanta?"

"I want to talk to you about that," he said. Out of the corner of his eye, he saw the waitress returning. "Later."

"Here we are," the woman said, quickly and efficiently plopping down two mugs of steaming black coffee, cream, sugar, two tall glasses of ice water and a bottle of aspirin.

"You're a jewel," Tate said, reaching for the aspirin.

"Nope. The name's Bessie." She waited until Tate had gulped down four aspirin. "You want some, too?" she asked, holding out the bottle to Maggie.

"No, thanks."

"Are you ready to order breakfast now, or do you want me to check back later?" Bessie asked.

Maybe it was the smell of the coffee that did it. Or the delicious scents and sounds coming from the kitchen—bacon frying, bread toasting, eggs sizzling. Tate was suddenly ravenously hungry. Salivating.

"I'm not hungry," Maggie said quickly.

Glancing across the table at her, Tate knew she was lying. "It's like this, Bessie," he said, reaching into his pocket, pulling out all his change, spreading it onto the table, then retrieving one quarter. "I need to save this for a phone call," he said.

"And this," he said, gesturing to the coins, "is all the money we have. I think it's enough to cover coffee, aspirin and your tip, but that's about it."

"Looks like more than that to me," Bessie said, starting to push the coins into little piles. "There's for the coffee. The aspirin's free... to everybody," she added, continuing to push the coins around. "We have a nice ninety-nine-cent special that includes two eggs, grits, biscuits and jelly. I'll bring an extra plate and you two can share.

"There's for the tax," she said, making another little pile of coins and counting the rest. "And it still leaves a little left over for my tip."

"Not much left over," Tate said.

"I didn't get into this line of work to get rich," Bessie said, placing her hand on her hip. "And I don't have all day, either. My shift ends in fifteen minutes. What do you say?"

"It's a deal," Tate breathed.

"Right," Bessie said, scooping up the coins, then waving her hand in the air as she waddled away.

Tate looked across the table at Maggie. She lifted her mug of coffee in a toast. "To Bessie," she said.

Tate touched his mug to hers and they both drank. "Mmm," he said. "This just might be the best coffee I ever had."

"Me, too." Maggie took another sip. She sighed. "What was it you were going to tell me about getting back to Atlanta?"

Tate frowned. "I'll tell you the truth, Maggie. At this moment, I can't talk—or even think—about anything except eggs and grits and biscuits and jelly. Are you as hungry as I am?"

She swallowed. "I think so. I'm almost sure of it."

They drank their coffee in silence until Bessie returned.

Tate saw Maggie's blue eyes widen even before their waitress got to the table. "Here you are, folks," Bessie said. "The special."

It was more than a special. It was a feast.

There were scrambled eggs, light and fluffy, at least five or six of them rather than the promised two, Tate noticed. And there was a huge mound of buttered grits, so hot he could see steam still rising from them. The eggs and grits took up an entire plate, so Bessie had brought the biscuits—at least half a dozen of them, lightly browned and obviously homemade—in a separate basket. And there was real butter. And three different kinds of homemade jellies—peach, strawberry and grape. And a whole platter of sizzling pink ham.

"The damn cook made a mistake," Bessie said, gesturing to the ham. "But I can't take it back. It's against government regulations. You can just leave it if you can't eat it."

Finally, Bessie plopped a full pot of coffee onto the table. "Free refills come with the food, but like I told you before, it's time for my shift to end. I gotta get home and get ready for church. I left your bill—marked paid in full—for the next waitress. Hope you don't mind my leaving you like this."

Tate shook his head, feeling a huge lump in his throat. "I said it right the first time, Bessie," he said. "You are a jewel. One of the best."

She brushed the compliment aside as if swatting a fly. "You take care now. You hear?"

Tate nodded as Bessie left. He looked across the table at Maggie and saw that her eyes were filled with tears. "What can you say?" he said.

She shrugged. "Let's eat?"

"IT'S LIKE THIS," Tate said, leaning back against the booth after he and Maggie had devoured everything in sight and were polishing off the rest of the coffee. "After you went to sleep last night, I got to thinking about what you'd said earlier."

She narrowed her eyes. "I said a lot of things last night, as I remember. Some of which I probably shouldn't have said. Is that what you're talking about?"

"You were right on target in this particular case. You nailed me."

"What did I say?"

"You accused me of being a quitter... of giving up before I'd exhausted all the possibilities."

"I said that?"

"Not in those exact words. But I got your message."

"And that message was...?"

"That I shouldn't go back to Atlanta, at least not right away. That I should follow my own convictions, my own instincts, and see this thing through. I'm going to do it, Maggie."

She took a deep breath, her mind racing but hopelessly lost. She cleared her throat. "And what is it exactly that you're going to do, Tate?"

"I'm going to expose the so-called financial consortium that's trying to take over the SCFC for the bunch of crooks they really are!"

"You are? How?"

"Well, I haven't worked out all the particulars yet. But I know they're supposed to own a processing plant near Panama City, Florida, not too far from here, and another one in Birmingham, Alabama. I'm going to visit those plants personally, undercover, and find out exactly what's going on. If those guys are as crooked as I believe they are, I'll find out enough to hang the lot of them."

"Hang?"

"Figuratively speaking. At least I'll find enough to force the SCFC board to send them on their way forever."

Maggie thought furiously. "So, what it boils down to is . . . you're not going back to Atlanta anytime soon."

"Right. I hadn't planned any of this when I stormed out of the meeting yesterday. I just wanted to get away from the whole mess. But things snowballed, and suddenly here I am on the road, with nobody knowing where I am. It's a fantastic opportunity."

She shook her head. "I don't follow your reasoning."

"I'll be on my own, free to make my own decisions again. At least until I decide to go back, or until they catch up to me. But by that time, I'll have the proof I need to expose the consortium."

"What happens if it doesn't work out that way? What happens if they aren't crooked, after all? Or if you can't find the proof you need to convince your board of directors that they are crooked?"

"At least I'll have tried. And that's a helluva lot better than giving up without a fight."

Maggie took a deep breath and slowly let it out. "You still have problems," she pointed out.

"I know."

"You have no money."

"And no credit cards," Tate added. "They were lost along with my wallet, but I wouldn't be able to use them anyway. If I tried to, the whole world would be able to find me in a matter of hours."

"So how will you live while you're tracking down the crooks and exposing them?"

"I'll make my own way. Manual labor, if need be. This is peach country, height of the season. I'm sure I'll be able to get a job at an orchard."

"That's only for a few weeks. What happens after that?"

"I should be in Panama City by then. I have a friend there who owns a bar on the beach. He'll be able to fix me up with something—waiting tables, scrubbing floors, whatever."

"You're really serious about this."

"I've never been more serious."

Maggie squinted her eyes and looked at him. "Really and truly?"

"Absolutely."

She thought about all he'd told her, then nodded. "I think you'll make it, Tate. I really believe you'll succeed."

"Thank you."

"I only have one suggestion to enhance your chances."

"What's that?"

Maggie hesitated for a fraction of a second. "Take me with you." She held her breath while she waited for his explosion.

It didn't come. Instead, he studied her quietly, thoughtfully, for a long time. "I don't think that's a good idea," he said at last.

"Why not?"

"I've told you how I'll be living. By the skin of my teeth. That's no life for you."

"I'm adaptable. Strong, too. I can earn my own keep."

"Working in a peach orchard from dawn to dusk?"

"If necessary. If that's the only job available."

He shook his head. "I'm sorry, Maggie."

"And there's something else. Two things."

"What?"

"Sooner or later—probably sooner—your family is going to have somebody out looking for you. But they'll be after one person, a man. They won't be searching for a couple."

Tate frowned. "And what's the other thing?"

"I have twenty dollars in my shoe."

He blinked. "You what?"

"I keep a twenty-dollar bill in my shoe for emergencies. And, as far as I'm concerned, taxi fares don't qualify, but I think this does, don't you?"

"Maggie," he chided, shaking his head.

"So, what do you say?"

Tate leaned forward in the booth and propped his elbows on the table, serious again. "What I don't understand is why you'd want to come with me. Why you'd even consider it."

"Because I'm mad about you?"

"Not good enough. Try again."

She sighed. "It was the mention of your friend that convinced me I should come along with you."

"My friend?"

"The one who owns the bar on the beach at Panama City, remember?"

"Yeah. What about him?"

"I was hoping he might give me a job singing . . . or introduce me to somebody who did need a singer."

"Oh," Tate said, slapping his forehead as he suddenly understood.

"Exactly," Maggie said. "I've heard about Panama City and the tons of tourists that flock down there every summer. It might be a golden opportunity, just what I've been looking for. At the very least, it's worth a shot. There's nothing for me back in Atlanta except a few personal items."

Tate winced. "I'm sorry as hell about causing you to lose your job."

She shrugged. "Here's your chance to make it up to me." Watching him closely, she could tell that he was wavering. "Besides," she added, playing her trump card, "if you don't take me with you, what happens to me? Surely you wouldn't leave me stranded alone out here in the middle of nowhere."

"You still have your twenty dollars."

She didn't even bother replying to that.

"Okay," Tate said. "I guess you can come with me. But don't say I didn't warn you about how tough it might be."

"I won't," she replied happily. Then she thought of something. "What *did* you plan to do with me if I hadn't suggested coming with you? Were you really going to leave me in this godforsaken hole?"

"You're not the only one with hidden resources, Maggie. Mine happens to be on my wrist," he said, holding up his arm.

"Your watch?"

"Not just a watch. A Rolex. Given to me in appreciation by a grateful board of directors a few years back. I'm going to pawn it and use the money to help me discredit my brother and make the board grovel."

Maggie laughed out loud. "Seems appropriate to me."

"I thought so, too. Shall we go look for a pawnshop?"

"Not today, Tate," she said, shaking her head. "If Planters' Junction is anything like the little town where I grew up in South Carolina, on Sunday the whole place is closed up tighter than a tick."

"Damn. I hadn't thought about that."

"See how lucky you are to have me with you?" she said, getting up from the booth.

"Not to mention your twenty dollars," he said, getting up, too.

Tate held the door open for her and Maggie stepped out into the bright sunshine. The blistering heat almost took her breath away. She was hit, too, by the sudden realization that Tate hadn't been exaggerating the discomforts that might lie ahead if she accompanied him in his undertaking. Maybe she should back out now...tuck in her tail and go home.

No! something inside her screamed. Tate wasn't the only one who wasn't a quitter. She'd come too far, sacrificed too much, to give up her dream of finding success as a singer without giving it this last, final shot. And this probably would be her last shot. She'd depleted her savings, and if nothing worked out for her in Panama City...

"Whew!" Tate said. "Feels like a real scorcher, and it's not quite noon yet."

"You think this is hot? You should feel South Carolina hot."

"I meant to ask you about that. From your accent, I thought you were a Yankee."

"A Yankee who can put away grits like I just did? C'mon. And besides, I do imitations, remember?"

"I'd forgotten," he admitted. "How'd you learn to do that?"

"It's a long story. I'll tell you someday. But in the meantime . . . what next?"

"These clothes make us stand out like sore thumbs," he said, taking off his suit jacket. "I'd planned to pawn the watch, go to the store and buy something casual. But I guess all the clothes stores will be closed today, too."

Maggie thought for a moment. "Maybe somebody's having a yard sale!"

"Huh?"

"They sell all kinds of things at yard sales—clothes, furniture, you name it. And people usually have them on weekends. Let's ask." Without waiting for a reply, Maggie walked over to the attendant manning the gas pumps at the truck stop.

"Hi," she said. The attendant was a teenager, and his face turned a bright red as soon as he looked around and saw her. It was really rather flattering, Maggie thought, hoping Tate was watching the young man's reaction, too.

"We were wondering whether somebody around here was having a yard sale today," she said. "Do you know of one?"

The young man nodded, and his face turned an even deeper red.

"Wonderful!" Maggie said. "Where is it?"

The attendant's Adam's apple bobbed up and down when he swallowed. "Miz Smith's house. On Madison Street."

"Madison Street," Maggie repeated. "And that's... over that way?" she asked, making a wild guess and pointing to her right.

The attendant nodded. "Two blocks south, then one block west."

"Thanks a lot," Maggie said, giving him her brightest smile and receiving an appropriate response. "You're a dear." She retraced her steps to Tate and saw the twinkle in his good eye, the one that wasn't red and swollen.

"You should be ashamed of yourself," he commented.

Maggie giggled. "Let's go find the yard sale as soon as I get the money out of my shoe."

The walk to Mrs. Smith's yard sale was a lot longer than the gas station attendant had indicated. "My feet are killing me," Maggie said.

"I can see why," Tate said, looking at her spiky high heels. "You want me to carry you?"

"What? You think we're not attracting enough attention already?" Several cars had slowed down while local drivers openly took stock of the two strangers in town— one dressed in a seductive black dress and the other sporting a black eye.

"We could stop and rest for a minute," Tate suggested.

Maggie shook her head. "It can't be much farther."

As soon as they turned the next corner, they spotted the sale in progress at a house about halfway down the block. "What do you think we'll need in the way of clothes?" Maggie asked.

"First, let's see what we can afford," Tate replied grimly.

They sauntered into the yard where a dozen or so people were milling about, and casually started inspecting the merchandise. Maggie picked up a plate with a crack running down the middle. She turned it over to check the price. "Ten cents," she whispered.

Tate held up a mug with the handle missing. "Five cents."

"Not bad."

He snorted. "It's a bunch of junk. They should be giving it away."

"Let's mosey over to the clothes," Maggie said quickly.

With a sinking feeling, she eyed the women's clothing arranged on hangers suspended from a clothesline. Almost everything she saw was outdated, faded, torn or all three. She did find one pair of khaki shorts that looked about her size and were priced at only a dollar and fifty cents.

Holding the shorts in her hand, she walked over to a nearby table where Tate was rummaging through men's clothing. "Any luck?" she asked.

"Not much," he said, holding up a pair of men's trousers at least three sizes too big for him. "I figure the guy who owned these must be a sumo wrestler."

Maggie snickered. Then she started sorting through jeans and finally came up with a pair that looked about the right size for her. "Only two dollars," she said excitedly. "Let's look for some for you."

They finally located a pair of jeans, a little worn but clean, that would fit him, and a couple of T-shirts for each of them. "Let's see," Maggie said, adding up the cost of their selections. "That comes to seven...eight... Nine-fifty, total. Not bad, wouldn't you say?"

"Mmm," he replied noncommittally. "But we still need shoes. Especially you."

Maggie also would have loved a spare set of underwear—not that she was keen on the idea of wearing someone else's panties—but didn't see any for sale. She made a mental note to look for a K-mart or ten-cent store as soon as possible.

They found a pair of high-top sneakers in Tate's size right away, but none that would fit Maggie. "They're all way too big," Tate said after they'd rummaged through the entire table.

"I have to have something!" Maggie declared with alarm.

"I dunno," Tate drawled. "Maybe you could braid your hair and go barefoot. I think you'd look sort of cute."

"Let's go through the stack again." They were still unable to find her size. "These are the smallest I saw," she finally said, holding up a pair of gray sneakers. "I'll just have to stuff paper in the toes."

Mrs. Smith was reluctant to allow them in her house, but after Maggie threatened to leave without buying anything if she wouldn't allow them to try on the merchandise first, the woman relented, showing them to separate bedrooms.

A little later, Tate and Maggie met in the hallway. They were both wearing their new purchases. "Jeans, T-shirts and sneakers," she said. "We could be twins."

"Not quite," he observed, lifting his eyebrows as he pointedly glanced at her rounded hips encased in the snug-fitting jeans.

Maggie felt a surge of pleasure. "I think these were made for a boy. They aren't too tight, are they?"

"They're just perfect. Perfect," he repeated. He cleared his throat. "Would you really have walked away if Mrs. Smith hadn't let us inside to dress?"

Maggie grinned. "What do you think?"

He shook his head. "You're something else, Maggie."

"Tell me about it," she said, looping her arm with his, "while we go outside to pay up."

Mrs. Smith reluctantly gave them a paper bag to carry the clothes they weren't wearing. "Do you happen to know of a peach orchard close by?" Tate asked her. "One where they might be hiring?"

"No," Mrs. Smith replied tersely.

"Sure you do, Lucy," another woman said. "Miller's Peach Orchard, right down the road." She turned to Tate. "Their Georgia Belles are coming in like crazy and they're practically begging for help. Pay right good wages, too, from what I've heard."

"How far is it?" Tate asked the woman.

"Go one block over and turn right. Can't be no more'n four or five miles."

"Thank you," Tate said, extending his hand.

"Good luck to you," the woman said, accepting his handshake.

Maggie waited until they were well away from the Smith house. "This town sure has all kinds."

"Most places do," Tate agreed. "Do you feel up to a little walk in the country?"

Maggie stopped in her tracks. "Where were you thinking about going?"

"In the direction of the Miller place. I thought we'd look out along the way for a place we can spend the night."

Maggie swallowed. "Spend the night? What kind of place?"

"A nice big shade tree. Or a deserted barn. Something like that."

Chapter Five

"You expect us to spend the night under a tree?" Maggie said hoarsely. "Or in a deserted barn?"

Tate nodded. "Unless you have a better idea. We sure don't have enough money for a motel. Not that I've seen one in Planters' Junction anyway."

He could tell from her reaction that she hadn't fully realized until now exactly what "roughing it" on their journey would entail. She'd probably had some misguided notion of a grand adventure without bothering to think about the nitty-gritty basics of life on the road, on the run. That's why he'd decided to test her mettle now, early on.

He still wasn't quite sure why he'd agreed to let her come with him in the first place, although her reasoning that he'd be less likely to be spotted with a female companion had something to do with it. Also, if he could help her career along—or at least help her land a singing job and get on her feet again—it would ease his guilt at her having lost her job at the Green Lantern.

And there was something else... another reason, a purely selfish one that he didn't want to explore but couldn't ignore, either. He enjoyed her company. He couldn't allow that to influence things, though.

"There is one other possibility," Tate said, looking to give her a graceful way out. "I noticed that the truck stop where we ate is also the bus station, and stays open twenty-four hours. We can camp out there tonight. First thing tomorrow, I'll pawn my watch, buy you a bus ticket to anywhere you want to go and give you some money to get started again. How does that sound?"

Maggie pursed her lips while she thought. "Sounds like you're trying to get rid of me," she said finally.

"I'm trying to do what you want, Maggie. And what's best for you."

She frowned. "If I go home now, back to where my folks live in South Carolina, I'll never get the nerve again to try for a singing career."

"You might."

"No. I know myself. I'd live the rest of my life in that little town. I'd die there . . . in more ways than one." She took a deep breath and let it out slowly. "I'd like to come with you, Tate. If you'll still let me."

Tate swallowed. He admired her courage. "I'd be honored," he said humbly.

They started walking again.

"The sun's hot, isn't it?" Maggie said about half an hour later.

Tate nodded his head. He tried not to think about how hot he was, with the afternoon sun beating down on them as they walked along the shoulder of the asphalt highway that stretched out straight and flat as far as the eye could see, without a shade tree in sight. There were some scraggly pine trees at a distance from the road on both sides, but that was it.

"Really hot," Maggie said after another fifteen or twenty minutes.

"It sure is." Tate tried not to think about how thirsty he was, either.

"If I had a million dollars, I'd give it gladly right now for a glass of water. Make that two million if it had ice in it."

"It doesn't help to think about it," Tate said. "Or to complain."

"You call this complaining? You should hear me when I really get going."

"I can hardly wait."

They continued walking and Tate started getting concerned. He'd forgotten how flat and desolate South Georgia could be in places. Unless they found some shade and water soon, there was a real danger of heatstroke.

"Let's stop and rest awhile," he suggested a short time later.

"Rest where? In the middle of the highway?"

"How about under those pine trees over there?" he said, pointing to his right.

"They won't give much shade," she said.

"Better than none at all."

"Okay," she agreed, heading out across the open field. Tate followed her, wondering if there were rattlesnakes in this area.

They reached the clump of pine trees. "It actually is cooler here," Maggie said. "A little."

"You can have our sack to sit on," Tate offered, plopping the paper bag containing their clothes onto the ground beside a tree. He expected her to make a sarcastic remark but she didn't. Instead, she sat on the sack and leaned back against the tree, closing her eyes.

Tate felt a wave of guilt. He should have his head examined, dragging a woman out here like this, exposing her to all sorts of dangers and hardships. And actually, she hadn't complained much at all.

"This is heavenly," Maggie breathed after a moment.

Tate felt even more guilty.

Then he heard something. He waited, holding his breath. Then he heard the sound again. "That sounded like a cow," he said in a loud stage whisper.

Maggie opened her eyes and leaned forward. "What did? I didn't hear anything."

"Listen." He held up his hand for silence, and waited. Nothing.

"I'm sure I heard a cow," he said finally.

"So?" she said, suppressing a yawn as she leaned back again.

"I'm going to investigate. Do you want to come with me?"

"If it's all the same to you, I'll just stay here and rest. I've seen cows before."

Tate hesitated. "I'll be back in a few minutes. Stay where you are."

"Where would I go?" She closed her eyes again.

Tate headed off in the direction of the sound he'd heard. He hadn't wanted to arouse false hopes in Maggie, but he knew that cows congregated around water. If there was a cow nearby, there probably also was a pond or lake. Even if he and Maggie couldn't drink the water, they could at least cool themselves in it.

After a short time, he walked out of the small pine thicket where he'd left Maggie and into bright sunshine again. The heat hit him like a hot blanket suddenly thrown over his head. He could barely breathe. Forcing his discomfort from his mind, he plodded across the open field, heading for another pine thicket, beyond which there was a small rise in the otherwise flat surface.

Distances are deceiving. Especially flat ones, Tate thought when he finally reached the thicket and had to stop to rest. He was breathing hard and sweating profusely, possibly in danger of passing out from the choking heat. And what would happen to Maggie if he collapsed out here in the middle of nowhere? What would she do? What would become of her?

It had been a foolhardy thing for him to do, going off in search of some stupid cows. He was beginning to doubt that he'd heard them in the first place. And even if he had, there was no assurance that he'd find water when he found them.

He wavered, but finally decided to forge ahead... at least to find out what was on the other side of that rise. After a short rest, he started out again.

If anything, the going was even worse than before, because the grade was slightly uphill now, and the underbrush was more dense. He stumbled, fell, thought about rattlesnakes again and got up quickly. Finally, he reached the highest point and straightened, looking out at the scene before him.

In the distance, he saw a small cabin, overgrown with vines, probably abandoned. A short way from the house, there was a weathered barn, more than a little rundown, but possibly strong enough to offer them shelter for the night.

He shifted his gaze and saw the cows, a half dozen of them, gathered under a shade tree beside a small pond. He grinned. Soon he and Maggie could be cooling themselves in that same small pond. Then Tate's gaze settled on something else, in a clearing close to the pond, and he caught his breath. It was almost too good to be believed!

He suddenly couldn't wait to tell Maggie about the treasure he'd found. But first, he was going to jump into that pond long enough to cool himself so he wouldn't be in danger of suffering heatstroke before he could get back to her.

"I DON'T UNDERSTAND why you're being so secretive," Maggie said, following Tate as he led the way back to his discovery. "I'm glad you found the pond where we can swim and the barn where we can spend the night. Really, I am. But why won't you tell me about the 'secret treasure' as you call it?"

"You'll find out soon enough."

"Before or after I hurl my body into the pond to cool off?"

"Wait and see," he replied cryptically.

"I hate surprises," she said. "Not to mention the people who spring them."

"You won't hate this one."

"Dammit, Tate!"

"We're almost there," he said, holding out his hand to pull her the last few steps up the little hill. "There!" he added when they reached the top.

He saw Maggie take a quick appraisal of the pastoral scene spread out before them. He was sure she noticed the cows and that the farmhouse was overgrown with weeds and abandoned. The barn was dilapidated and the pond was small. He was relieved that she didn't comment on any of that. Instead, she let out a whoop, spread out her arms and started running down the hill.

"Last one in's a rotten egg!" she shouted, racing toward the pond.

"It's shallow!" Tate cautioned, throwing down their sack of clothes and taking off after her.

He wasn't sure she'd heard him. She must have, though, because she didn't dive in when she reached the water's edge. Instead, she spread out her arms again and fell into the water—clothes, shoes and all—making a gigantic splash.

Pausing only long enough to remove his sneakers, Tate followed her into the pond.

Maggie did a shallow, fishtail dive into the green water and came up seconds later, pushing back her wet hair as she lifted her face to the sun. After a moment, she dived again, a little deeper this time as she tested the water.

"Mmm," she said as soon as she came up. "It doesn't get any better than this."

Floating on his back while he watched her innocent delight, Tate had to agree. "You might enjoy it more if you took off your shoes," he commented.

"No way. I know how icky ponds are on the bottom. I'm not putting my bare feet in that gooey stuff."

"Chicken," he said with a laugh.

Maggie reached out her hand and pinched his toe. Tate gave an exaggerated shout of alarm before he rolled over and dived beneath the water, going after her. Maggie screeched satisfactorily before swimming away from him, heading for the deeper water in the middle of the pond.

Tate came up a moment for air and saw Maggie doing the same. They took each other's measure for a moment, then went back underwater at the same time. The battle began in earnest.

Tate tried to circle around her—the shark, silent and deadly—until Maggie unexpectedly pinched his ankle. He reversed direction, swam a short distance away, then returned from a different angle, catching her by surprise this time. He grabbed her arm with one hand and used his other to propel them to the surface.

"Gotcha!" he said. He gave her a couple of seconds to catch her breath. Then he dunked her head in the water. She came up sputtering. "Give up?" She shook her head; he dunked her again.

She raised her hand in surrender when he let her up next time. Then, unexpectedly, she slid her arm around his shoulder, bringing her face close to his. Surprised for a moment, Tate quickly recovered, pulling her closer to him with one arm while he treaded water with the other. He wasn't sure who made the next move, but suddenly they were kissing.

Her lips were wet and cool from the water, and when they parted for him, her mouth was warm and sweet inside. He felt her other arm go around his neck, and wondered how much longer he could keep them both afloat. Then he felt her legs wrapping around his waist, felt her settle herself against his groin...and he no longer wondered. He no longer cared about anything except the touch and taste of her—her legs around him, her arms around him, her hands all over him...*pushing him under the water?*

She was. She did. When he came up sputtering a few seconds later, she was several feet away. Laughing.

"I got you that time!" she said triumphantly.

"So you did," he said. "How about a rematch?"

She shook her head and headed for shore. "My clothes are so waterlogged, it's hard to swim."

"You could always take them off."

"In your dreams, Rabun," she said with a laugh.

Tate followed her out of the pond. "Are you ready for your surprise now?"

"I'd almost forgotten!" Maggie said. "What is it?"

Taking her hand, he led her to a shade tree some distance from the cows. "Have a seat," he said. Maggie sat down. "No, face that way," he said, pointing to the left. "And don't turn around to peek."

Maggie shifted around. "This better be good."

"It is." Tate hurried off, and was back with his treasure in less than a minute. "You can turn around now," he said.

She did, and her eyes widened. She scrambled to her knees. Her mouth opened and closed. She swallowed.

Tate grinned, waiting for her to find her voice.

Her tongue darted out to moisten her lips. "A watermelon!" she finally whispered.

Tate nodded, then told her reverently, "There's a whole patch of them on the other side of the pond. A whole patch!"

Maggie closed her eyes.

Tate busted the watermelon against the tree. He handed an entire half to Maggie, keeping the other half for himself. They ate it with their fingers, barely talking as they ate, savoring the sweet meat and letting the juices fall where they chose—through their fingers, down their chins, onto their clothes.

"We can jump into the pond to wash off when we're finished," Tate said.

"Mmm," Maggie said, nodding her agreement. She held up a chunk of red melon, opened her mouth wide, then dropped the morsel inside.

Tate watched as her pink lips closed around the tasty tidbit, and he felt a sudden surge of sexual excitement in his loins. He shifted his gaze back to the melon he was eating. He didn't think Maggie was deliberately trying to arouse him. It was probably the furthest thing from her mind. He wondered what might happen if she actually did try to excite him.

After they'd eaten melon and cleaned themselves in the pond afterward, they sat in the sun to dry their clothes. Maggie made a halfhearted attempt to plait her hair while Tate lay on the ground watching her. "It won't stay this way long without a ribbon or something to hold it," she said when she'd finally managed a braid.

"I think it looks great. Sexy."

"You think about sex a lot, don't you?"

"Only when I'm around you."

She rolled her eyes.

"Have you ever been married, Maggie?"

"No." She looked at him. "Have you?"

"Nope. Engaged?"

There was a moment's hesitation. "Yes. Have you?"

"Nope," he repeated.

"Any particular reason?"

"Too busy working, I guess," he said. "And I never seemed to meet the right woman—one I couldn't live without."

"You think that's a requirement? That you can't live without a certain person?"

Tate rubbed the stubble on his face. "I think that feeling that way is a good beginning." He thought she might challenge him on that, but she didn't. "What happened?" he asked after a moment. "With your engagement, I mean."

"That's getting a little personal, don't you think?"

"Yes. And you can tell me to mind my own business, if you want to." He watched her, and thought for a while that she was going to do exactly that. He could tell the exact moment when she changed her mind, and fleetingly wondered how he was able to read her so well, considering the short time they'd known each other.

"We'd been high school sweethearts," she said. "I was a cheerleader. He was captain of the football team. It's an old story and you can stop me if you've heard it a hundred times before."

"Nobody's stopping you," he said.

"After high school, Royce—that was his name—won a football scholarship to Clemson. We talked about getting married then, but our families, especially his, talked us out of it. So Royce went off to Clemson. I took a secretarial course, got a job and lived at home in order to save money for when we got married.

"Royce became a big football star at Clemson. Well, not that big, but pretty big. And I was as thrilled as he was when the Chicago Bears drafted him. I thought we should get married right away, but Royce said we should wait a year...give him time to make a place for himself in the NFL.

"So we waited a year. Then it was two years. And then he married somebody else. A stewardess he met in Chicago."

Tate rolled over onto his stomach and looked up at her. She was gazing into the distance, far beyond the cows. Neither of them spoke. Tate finally cleared his throat. "You know something, Maggie? I always thought football players were dumb," he said. "Now I'm sure of it."

She shifted her clear blue eyes, focusing on him. After a long moment she smiled. "Thanks for that."

"You're welcome." He thought for a moment. "But how did you get from there to here? When did you leave home and set out to become a singer? And how did you learn to imitate voices the way you do?''

She smiled again. ''The voices were the easy part. I was in the glee club in high school, and the choral director was a frustrated stand-up comic. She taught all of us the basics of recognizing and imitating certain inflections in the voice, and using mannerisms to build on that. She said I had a natural talent.''

''You do. What about the rest?''

''After Royce . . . uh . . . made his sneaky maneuver, I noticed that people in our hometown were looking at me in a different way. I was no longer the so-called golden girl—the high school cheerleader engaged to the handsome, successful football hero. Suddenly I was on the shelf. Over the hill. A twenty-five-year-old spinster with no prospects. Men I'd never even seen before started crawling out from under their rocks to ask me out on dates.''

Tate laughed. ''You're exaggerating.''

''Only a little. But I still stayed around for a while longer because I didn't know what else to do with myself. For as long as I could remember, I'd had only one goal—marriage and raising a family with Royce. Now all of that was gone . . . just like that.'' She snapped her fingers.

''I might have stayed in that little nothing town, feeling sorry for myself for the rest of my life, but then . . . something really wonderful happened to me.''

Tate sat up. ''What was that?''

''I lost my job.''

''You call that wonderful?''

"It was! It got me off my rear end. The company I'd been working for sold out to a big outfit in Chicago. They gave me the option of transferring there—and you can guess how I'd feel about going to Chicago and possibly someday running into Royce and his wife—or accepting a nice severance bonus."

"You took the money and ran," Tate said.

"You bet. And don't forget the money I'd saved up all those years living at home. I decided it was time for me to go after something strictly for me for a change. I decided to take my savings and go on the road and become a singing star. A big success. I'd show them all—my folks, Royce and his folks, the whole town."

She took a deep breath and let it out with a whoosh. "It didn't quite work out that way."

"What happened?"

"First of all, I decided to try my luck in Athens, Georgia. A lot of good music was coming out of there about that time—the B-52's, Indigo Girls, R.E.M. Great sounds. But after a few tryouts, I agreed with the producers I met. The music wasn't right for me.

"So I headed for another college town, Austin, Texas. I got a job waiting tables and singing country-western, and did pretty well, too. After about a year, though, I got restless. And greedy. So I went to Nashville, where I didn't do well at all. Let me tell you, that place is *crawling* with would-be singers. Not only couldn't I get an audition, I couldn't even get a job waitressing.

"I finally met another singer, Joyce, who had a manager. He talked the two of us into doing a sister act, and booked us into a series of one-night stands." Maggie shook her head and laughed. "I tell you, we sang in every podunk town from Tennessee to Texas, a new place every night. It was quite an experience.

"Joyce finally said she'd had enough of riding buses and living out of suitcases to last a lifetime, and was heading for Atlanta. I was pretty sick of the road myself, so I went along with her. First thing she did when we got there, though, was to call up an old flame of hers. Before you could blink an eye, the two of them had gone off and gotten married...with her still owing the landlord her share of the rent money."

"So that's how you happened to get locked out of your apartment?"

Maggie nodded. "She must have started feeling bad about leaving me stuck the way she did, because she called day before yesterday. She said she'd fixed me up with a job at the Green Lantern, and that a big record producer would be there to catch my act."

"But I showed up before you had a chance to meet him," he said, shaking his head.

"I doubt that there even was a record producer, Tate. I certainly didn't see anybody who looked like one... except you."

He shook his head again. "That's some story."

"As they say in the movies, you should have been there."

"How long have you been away from home now?" he asked.

"Three years. Which makes me twenty-nine, in case you wondered."

"I did. And I'm thirty-four...in case you wondered."

"I did," she admitted with a laugh.

"So tell me, twenty-nine-year-old Maggie. What do you think of our own little road trip so far?"

She didn't hesitate. "It's been a laugh and a thrill a minute. And I'll tell you something else, Tate. I think that both of us just might find what we're looking for on this trip. You'll get the proof you need to expose those crooks and get your company back, and I'll be on my way to a big-time singing career. I really have a good feeling about it."

"I hope you're right, Maggie. On both counts." He glanced at his watch. "But right now, I think we should take a look at that barn to see if we want to spend the night there."

"So soon?" Maggie asked, her reluctance obvious.

"We'll be able to see it better in the daylight. And we'll still have time to look for another place if it's totally uninhabitable."

"I suppose you're right," Maggie said, getting to her feet.

"Maybe it won't be too bad, after all," he said, crossing his fingers for luck.

He should have crossed his toes, too, Tate decided a little later as he examined the inside of the barn. And possibly his eyes, as well. The place was dark, cavernous and musky, with cobwebs hanging from every rafter.

"We can't stay here!" Maggie said.

"It's not that bad."

"It's worse!"

"We shouldn't be too hasty," he said, trying to reassure her. And himself. "We need to take a good look around first."

"No thanks. I've seen all I want to see."

"C'mon, Maggie," he coaxed. "At least give me a chance to look around a little more."

She finally shrugged in resignation.

Tate quickly busied himself, searching desperately for ways to make the barn more habitable. He knew that the shelter, poor as it was, was safer than sleeping outside in the snake-infested countryside.

He found a pitchfork, and went around tearing down cobwebs while he looked for something...anything. "A blanket!" he exclaimed when he spied one hanging over the gate to one of the stalls. He shook it out, then proudly carried it over to Maggie.

"What do you think of this!" he said.

"It smells bad."

"We'll get used to it in no time."

Maggie eyed the blanket dubiously.

"I'm going to muck out one of the stalls," Tate said. "Then I'll bring in clean hay, spread it around and put the blanket on top of it. It'll be almost like sleeping in a feather bed."

"I don't know..." she said.

"At least, it'll be more comfortable than sleeping on the bare ground out in the open, with no telling what animals are roaming around," he pointed out.

That did it, he noticed with only the slightest twinge of guilt.

"I'll take the blanket outside and shake it out some more," Maggie said.

"Great."

Tate worked furiously and by the time Maggie returned, the stall was in pretty good shape. She wordlessly handed him the blanket, then backed up a couple of steps and stood watching while he got down on his hands and knees to spread it out over the clean hay he'd arranged.

Finishing the job to his satisfaction, Tate was just about to get up when he heard a strangled sound coming from Maggie.

"What—?" he said, looking around to see what the matter was. He found himself staring into the twin barrels of a shotgun . . . one that was pointed directly at his head.

"You want to tell me who you are and what you're doing in my barn?" a steely voice said. "Or should I just go ahead and blow you to kingdom come right now?"

Chapter Six

Tate didn't move, and barely breathed. He could only stare at the apparition in front of him . . . the apparition holding a shotgun aimed at his head.

She was a little old lady—barely more than four feet tall, he guessed—dressed in an old-fashioned sunbonnet and a flowered print dress that came to her ankles. He was immediately struck by her uncanny resemblance to a cartoon character he remembered from a comic strip he'd seen when he was a kid. She looked exactly like Mammy Yokum in "L'il Abner."

"Look—" Tate said, finally able to speak.

"I already done my looking," the old woman said. "Been watching you two for hours—carrying on in my pond, disturbing my cows, *stealing my watermelons!*"

"We only took one," Maggie said, speaking up at last.

"One's enough to send you to jail . . . unless I decide to shoot you first."

"The only reason we took it is that we were hungry and thirsty," Maggie said.

The woman narrowed her eyes. "You two seem well fed to me."

"She's telling the truth," Tate said, scrambling to his feet while Mammy Yokum's attention was on Maggie.

"That's far enough!" the woman said, tightening her finger on the trigger as she turned back to Tate.

"Sorry," Tate said.

"Make another move like that and it's all over for you right here and now."

"I won't move." He gestured his head in Maggie's direction. "But what she just told you is the honest truth. We walked out here today from Planters' Junction. We were hot and tired, and were just looking for a place to cool off. But then I saw your watermelon patch and... I'm sorry. We have some money. A little. We'll pay you for the melon."

"'Pears to me, you planned to help yourself to the use of my barn, too," the woman said, glancing pointedly to the makeshift bed Tate had arranged.

"That's true," Tate admitted.

"Why'd you come all the way out here in the first place?"

"We were hoping to find work at the peach orchard."

"Miller's?"

"That's the place."

"You won't find any today. They're closed on Sundays."

Tate nodded. "I thought if I could be there first thing tomorrow morning, I'd stand a better chance of getting a job."

The woman narrowed her eyes. "For how long?"

"Beg pardon?"

"How long you planning to work at Miller's?"

"Not long," Tate answered truthfully. "Just until we earn enough money to be on our way again."

"Where you headed?"

Tate shook his head. "I don't think I should tell you that. Somebody might come looking for us later, and you can't tell them where we went if you don't know your-self.''

"You kill somebody?"

"No. And we didn't rob anybody, either. Except for the melon we took from you." Then he suddenly remembered something. "Oh. I do owe some money to a cab driver back in Atlanta. But I plan to mail it to him later."

Tate automatically jumped back when she suddenly waved the shotgun in the direction of his eye.

"So how'd you get that?" she asked.

"An honest fight. In a bar," he added.

"That's your whole story?"

"No. But the rest is personal. It has to do with my family."

The woman thought for a spell and then nodded her head. "A feud."

"Not exactly." Thinking about it some more, Tate reconsidered his reply. "Well, sort of."

"What about her?" the woman asked, gesturing her head in Maggie's direction. "You two married?"

"Yes," Tate said.

"No," Maggie said at the same time.

"So which is it?" Mammy Yokum asked Tate.

"We're not married."

"You two need to get your stories straight."

"I guess so," he agreed.

The woman fell silent, obviously thinking things over. Both Tate and Maggie were silent, too. Tate fervently hoped the old lady would let them go on their way without further ado. That was about the best they could hope for.

"I don't give charity," Mammy Yokum finally said. "And I don't take charity."

Tate didn't know what to reply to that, so he merely nodded.

"But if you're willing to put in some good, honest labor, I have a few chores that need doing around the house."

A few chores? Tate thought with a sinking feeling. Didn't she realize that the whole place was falling in around her?

"If you do 'em to my satisfaction, you'll earn your keep and I'll let you stay here tonight on this nice pallet you made for yourself," she said, gesturing toward the blanket with her shotgun.

Tate took a deep breath. "What chores did you have in mind for me to do?"

"Some fence railing needs repairing, and the front porch to the house..."

"I wouldn't even be able to get to the front porch until I cut down a mess of vines. And from what I've seen of it at a distance, that's a full day's job in itself."

"So maybe you can stay here a couple of days, or even three or four."

"And what do Maggie and I eat in the meantime?" he asked, growing angry. "Seeing as how you begrudged us one measly watermelon."

"It weren't measly and you know it!"

"Okay. One watermelon. But the question still stands."

"I guess I could throw in breakfast and supper for the two of you. And make a sandwich for you to take to the Millers' while you're working at the orchard there."

Tate blinked. "Let me get this straight. You expect me to work at Miller's orchard, and do all that work for you around here at the same time?"

"You said you wanted to earn money, didn't you? And I'm sure not going to pay you more than room and board to do a few simple chores. Besides, the orchard always shuts down by six in the afternoon, and there's plenty of daylight hours left after that...unless you think you're not man enough to work a full day."

"I'm plenty man enough!"

"But you're lazy. Right?"

"*No!* I'm not lazy!" Tate shouted, and was immediately chagrined that he'd let the old lady get to him. She was a sly fox, that one, and had neatly maneuvered him into saying exactly what she wanted him to say. And probably into doing exactly what she wanted him to do, as well.

"'Course, there is the matter of your lady friend here," the old woman said.

"Maggie?" Tate whispered hoarsely. "What about her?"

"The Millers don't hire women at the orchard. They say it causes too much trouble."

"I'm not sure I believe you at this stage," he said.

The woman shrugged. "Suit yourself. You can have her trudge all the way over there tomorrow for nothing if you want to."

"Or...?"

"Or she can stay here with me and help earn her keep."

"Doing what?" Tate said from between clenched teeth. "Slave labor?"

Mammy Yokum snorted. "Woman's work around the house. Easy chores. So what do you say?"

Tate looked at Maggie for the first time since he'd come unglued, and was astonished to see that she was trying to suppress her laughter. How could she possibly find all this amusing?

"I'll leave the decision up to Maggie," he said, throwing the ball into her court and daring her to return it.

"I say we stay," she replied without hesitation. "By all means."

Tate couldn't believe she'd said that. He shifted his eyes back to the old woman behind the shotgun, which she still held trained on him. "I guess that's it," he said, spreading his hands out helplessly.

"I told you not to move!" the woman shouted, pulling the trigger while Tate watched in hopeless horror.

The trigger clicked.

Nothing else happened.

No loud boom when the shotgun went off. No searing pain when the bullets entered his body. No nothing.

Except for the crone cackling with laughter.

"What happened?" Tate asked in a whisper barely loud enough to be heard above the hammering of his heart.

"No bullets!" the woman said, still laughing as she turned around and headed out of the barn. "Haven't had any to fit this shotgun in years."

Tate took a deep breath. Another one. He reached up and wiped the sweat off his forehead. Maggie came up to him. She looked at him for a long time, then she shook her head.

"First Bessie at the truck stop, and now Mammy Yokum," she said. "I'll say one thing for you, Tate Rabun. You sure have a way with women."

THE OLD LADY'S NAME was Granny Fortson. And she wasn't nearly as tough as she'd first appeared to be today, Maggie decided. Of course, the fact that Granny wasn't wielding a shotgun now might have something to do with causing Maggie to change her mind.

Still, even though Granny Fortson was bossy and set in her ways, she had a sense of humor, which was always a plus in Maggie's book. Granny told Tate to give first priority to shoring up the split rail fencing, rather than cutting down vines and repairing the front porch. She gave him a hammer and bucket of nails, and led the way to the pasture.

"Keeping the fence up means money in the bank," she said. "But the front porch is vanity. Pure vanity."

"It's also the way people come in and out of your house," he pointed out.

"There's a perfectly good door in the back. Friends know about it, and strangers don't have no business knowing about it."

"Where does the money from keeping up the fence come in?" Maggie asked.

"From Tom Mooney," Granny Fortson replied, cackling with delight. "After my husband, Ben, died about two years back, Tom came over here and bought all our milk cows. Paid good money for 'em, too. Cash money. And now he pays me every month, regular as clockwork, to let them same cows graze on my land. 'Course in bad weather, they need to sleep in the barn," she added pointedly.

"Of course," Tate replied. "But you don't get too much bad weather down here."

"Hardly none a'tall," Granny agreed, nodding her head. "But you ain't heard the best of it yet. Tom Mooney still gives me all the milk I can use. Truth be told, it's more than I can use. I churn every now and then when I got too much milk on my hands, and sell off the butter. Now, don't that beat all?"

"Sure does," Maggie said.

"Sounds like you're one smart businesswoman," Tate added.

Granny Fortson narrowed her eyes. "I'm smart enough to know when somebody's buttering me up, like you are right now, instead of doing their honest chores the way I'm paying 'em to do."

Tate sighed. "What do I do? Just follow this railing and fix everything that needs fixing?"

"That's all," Granny Fortson said.

"See you in a couple of months," Tate whispered to Maggie before he sat down the bucket of nails and started hammering.

"What did he whisper to you?" Granny said as she and Maggie headed back to the farmhouse.

"He said he'd see us at suppertime," Maggie replied quickly.

"Hmmph! I guess he expects a big hot meal."

"Probably not," Maggie said, although she had no idea what Tate's eating habits actually were.

"I ought to have my head examined," Granny Fortson said. "Big strapping young man like him will probably eat me out of house and home."

"I'm sure that won't happen."

"Well, come on with you now. We need to pick something from the garden and get started cooking. I know how hungry these men can be when they come home from working in the field."

It was then, at that exact moment, that Maggie knew with certainty how much Granny Fortson was enjoying this whole thing. Tough as she was, the old lady was lonely. And she was relishing the prospect of feeding Tate, big strapping young man that he was.

The garden, located in a big patch behind the farmhouse, was overflowing with fresh, succulent treasures—tomatoes, corn, squash, okra, green beans, peas, cucumbers, butter beans... There was no telling what else might be hidden beneath the weeds that were rapidly overtaking everything.

"Did you plant all this yourself?" Maggie asked.

"Yep. Same as always."

"It's magnificent," Maggie said with awe. "But maybe I should take time tomorrow to pull out some of the weeds?"

"I had in mind for us to start making cucumber pickles," Granny replied with a frown.

"The sweet, crisp kind?"

Granny nodded.

"I love those pickles. My grandmother used to make them."

"If you ever seen her make 'em, you know it takes about three to four days. But I guess you can pull up a few weeds while we're waiting for 'em to soak in lime water. We'll need to be freezing some corn and green beans... and canning tomatoes, too, before they go bad."

Tate was right about Granny Fortson, Maggie decided after she made a few mental calculations. The old lady certainly didn't mind putting people to work for their keep.

She didn't stint on the food she served them, either, Maggie noted as she helped Granny cut, clean and cook the food for supper. By the time Tate came into the kitchen through the back door—long after dark—delicious aromas filled the big, old-fashioned room. There were the mouth-watering scents of warmed-over beef roast, fresh corn bread and myriad vegetables, not to mention the fresh peach cobbler bubbling happily in the oven. Granny Fortson had whipped that up for dessert at the last minute.

"Mmm," Tate said. "Something smells good enough to eat." He plopped a stainless steel bucket onto the kitchen counter. "I met Tom Mooney's boy up at the milk shed and he sent along this bucket of milk, too. I guess we'll eat high on the hog tonight."

"Nobody sets down to my table until they're washed up good and proper," Granny Fortson said, pointedly eyeing Tate's sweat-drenched face and T-shirt. "There's an outdoor shower on the side of the barn. My man Ben always made use of it afore he came into the house."

"Good idea," Tate said, nodding. "I'll be back in no time." He started for the door, but stopped after only a couple of steps. "Uh . . . you don't happen to have some soap, do you? And a towel?"

"I ought to have my head examined," Granny grumbled as she left the room. "I suppose you'll be wanting fancy bubble bath next."

"You doing okay?" Tate asked Maggie as soon as the old lady left.

"Fine. But you must be exhausted." He had to be, she thought, after all that had happened last night and today.

"I'll tell you the truth," he said with a grin. "I haven't felt this good since I can't remember when."

He wasn't kidding, Maggie realized with surprise. She looked around to make sure Granny hadn't returned yet. "Just remember to save me some of that soap. I'm planning on making use of that shower later tonight, too."

Granny returned with soap and a couple of well-worn towels. "One apiece," she said. "Just remember they're on loan and I expect 'em back clean as they are now."

"Yes, ma'am," Tate said. "Thank you. I'll be back in a minute."

While Tate was gone, Granny directed Maggie on where to find the dishes to set the table for supper. By the time she finished, he was back, his blond hair still wet from the shower, the stubble on his face even more pronounced, his damaged eye darkening into variegated hues of green and purple...

He was gorgeous.

His skin had turned golden in the sun today, and the hairs on his forearms were lighter. He'd changed into a clean T-shirt, too, Maggie noticed. She also noticed the width of his chest underneath the T-shirt and the way the faded jeans hugged his hips... and the healthy, clean, outdoorsy, all-male scent of him.

Maggie turned away, hoping that Granny Fortson hadn't noticed the way she was openly admiring her traveling companion, almost drooling over the masculine sight and smell of him. *Too late,* she thought when she heard Granny clear her throat. Maggie forced herself to turn around. She was totally surprised by the lively, mischievous gleam she saw in the old lady's eyes.

"We'd best get the food on the table while it's still fit to eat," Granny said.

The three of them did justice to the food, Maggie observed silently. She found the familiar flavors of the home-cooked meal irresistible after being on the road so long without them, and Tate was obviously ravenous after a hard day's work. Granny, too, ate a surprising amount considering her size and age, probably because she hadn't had anyone to eat with in such a long time.

"That was delicious," Tate said, putting down his paper napkin after taking the last bite of peach cobbler. "And I'm talking about everything on the table."

Granny nodded. "You can't beat fresh for good vittles."

"That's for sure," Tate agreed.

After they'd all finished, Maggie got up to clean the kitchen and Tate started to help, but Granny would have none of it. "This is woman's work," she said.

"So it is," he said, winking at Maggie behind the old lady's back. She made a face at him.

Tate sat back down at the kitchen table. Maggie put away the leftover food and washed the dishes. Granny Fortson gave instructions to Maggie while she gave advice to Tate, keeping up a running commentary.

"Twin brothers—Brice and Price Miller—own the orchard. The knives and forks go in the drawer beside the sink. Brice is the one you need to talk to—he's got the sense in the family."

"Okay," Tate said. "I'll ask to see Brice tomorrow morning when I apply for a job."

"No, no!"

"I shouldn't ask to talk to Brice?"

"The pots and pans go in the cabinet beside the sink, Maggie. Not *under* it." She turned back to Tate. "Are you deaf or something? Didn't I just tell you that you should ask for Brice?"

And so it went.

After the last of the dishes were put away to Granny's satisfaction, she told Maggie and Tate to stay put while she went to get a lantern, returning only seconds later with a battery-operated one. "Batteries are expensive, you know. And I'm expecting you to replace these before you leave."

"We could make do with a kerosene lamp," Tate suggested. "It would be a lot less expensive. If you have one."

"Humph! I got one, all right. Got several. But I wouldn't trust the two of you out in the barn with one, not for a minute."

"Why not?" Maggie asked.

"I seen the way you two look at each other. I know what you're liable to do out in my barn. Carrying on the way you'll be doing, there's no telling what you'll knock over. With a kerosene lamp, the whole place would be up in flames afore anybody knew what was happening."

"That's not—" Maggie started to protest.

"Not a bad idea," Tate interrupted. "A battery lantern sounds a lot safer to me, too."

"But—" Maggie said.

"I'm sure Maggie will agree with me after she's had a chance to think it over," Tate said. "No matter how much we carry on tonight, we won't be likely to start a fire and burn the barn down."

Grabbing Maggie's hand, he pulled her over to Granny Fortson. "We'll say good-night to you now," he said, leaning over to kiss the old lady's forehead before he gently removed the lantern from her hands.

Maggie opened her mouth again to protest.

"Say good-night, Maggie," Tate commanded.

She started to argue with him, but decided against it for the time being. "Good night," she said instead.

"Damn you, Tate Rabun!" she said as soon as they were safely outside, heading for the barn in the bright moonlight.

"Whatever for?" he asked, feigning innocence.

"You know very well what for! Leading that old woman on the way you did . . . leading her to think . . ."

"That we're lovers? She'd be thinking it no matter what I said to her. It's what she wants to believe."

"And what must she think of me!"

"That you have good taste in men?" He suddenly stopped walking. Since he was still holding her hand, Maggie had to stop, too. He stared at her for a moment. "Are you serious?"

"Of course I'm serious."

"You mean it really bothers you that Granny Fortson thinks we're sleeping together?"

Feeling slightly foolish, Maggie answered truthfully, "Yes."

"But why would you care one way or another what the old lady thinks?"

"If you must know the truth, she reminds me of my grandmother."

"And . . . ?"

"I—I don't want her to think of me . . . in that light."

"Oh." He suddenly released her hand. "I'm sorry, Maggie. I didn't realize."

"There's no way you could have," she said. "And don't tell me I'm being silly, because I already know I am."

"I wasn't going to say that."

There was more she needed to tell him to set things straight between them. "Look," she said, taking a deep breath. "I'm no saint. But in spite of the kind of life I lead, and the people I associate with . . ."

She deliberately paused, hoping that he'd help her out on this. He remained silent. Stolidly, forbiddingly silent. "I don't sleep around, Tate," she blurted out.

There was another long silence.

"Neither do I, Maggie," he finally said.

"I like you, like you a lot. But we only met last night. We barely know each other."

"I don't buy that," he said, taking her hand again. "And I don't think you really do, either. The two of us have shared more in twenty-four hours than a lot of people do in weeks. Months. I think we know each other very well. And I have to tell you, I like you a lot, too."

He squeezed her hand then. His was warm and strong, much larger than hers. Their hands fit perfectly, she thought crazily. And he was right. They did know each other already, in spite of the short time they'd spent together. She felt closer to him than anybody she'd known in years, perhaps in her entire life. She suddenly wanted him to kiss her again, the way he'd done last night and then at the pond today.

"Maggie," he said, pulling her into his arms as if he'd just read her thoughts. "I'm going to kiss you now."

Even though she'd wanted this, it wasn't supposed to happen. "Tate . . ."

"It's merely a kiss," he said softly, catching her lower lip between his, nibbling gently, then running his tongue along the smooth surface. "Don't read anything more into it than that."

Then his mouth covered hers, his lips firm and sure, insistent. She brought her hand up to push him away, but the hand strayed out of her control and ended up on his shoulder, stroking the corded muscles she felt beneath her fingertips. Her other hand found its way to the back of his head, where it buried itself in his thick soft hair.

It's merely a kiss, she told herself as his arm tightened around her back, holding her body against his. *Merely a kiss,* she repeated, tightening her arms around him. *Merely a kiss,* she echoed, feeling herself drowning in a sea of sensuous pleasure.

And then he lifted his head, looking down at her in the bright moonlight. "See? Just a kiss between old friends," he said. He kissed her again, hard, for a brief moment. "Nothing threatening about that, was there?"

"No," she whispered, knowing it wasn't true. Everything about her had felt threatened by his kiss. Her willpower. Her resolve. And most definitely her peace of mind.

He touched her cheek with the tips of his fingers. "And I'll tell you a secret," he murmured. "Flattering as it is, I think both you and Granny Fortson are overestimating my...uh...stamina."

"Oh?" Maggie said, looking up into his eyes and noticing that they were crinkling at the corners with amusement.

"Consider what's happened to me lately," he said, leaning away a little, but keeping his hands on her waist in a light embrace. "I drank a lot of booze last night. I got involved—heavily—in a barroom brawl. And then I jumped on a truck and ran away from home with the most attractive woman I've ever met. And that's just for starters."

Maggie giggled. She filed away his flattering description of her, keeping it in the back of her mind to haul out and savor later.

"Then today, after no sleep at all last night—"

"You didn't get *any* sleep?" she asked.

Tate shook his head. "I was afraid even to close my eyes. The driver could have stopped while we were both asleep and hauled the two of us off to jail."

"Poor Tate," Maggie said, gently touching her fingers to the tender skin above his battered eye.

"After that," he continued with a shrug, "everything else was a piece of cake. Conning breakfast with only a couple of bucks between us, or so I thought, and then going on a mad shopping spree after you suddenly produced that twenty from your shoe. And walking for miles in the hot sun, hoping to find a place to stay tonight."

"Not to mention hoping to find a job tomorrow," Maggie said, starting to laugh. "And then being accosted by a little old lady with a shotgun."

"A shotgun that I fully believed to be loaded," Tate added, laughing along with her.

"And having her actually pull the trigger on you!"

Tate groaned. "I tell you, Maggie, it's been quite a day."

"You forgot to mention working on the fence for hours."

"Oh, yeah. That, too." They both laughed again. "So, in spite of what Granny Fortson might think about my physical prowess, I'm no threat at all to you tonight."

Maggie gave an exaggerated sigh. "Is that a promise?"

"Do you want it to be?"

"For the time being, yes," she said, no longer quite so sure she meant what she was saying.

"I'll probably already be asleep by the time you finish your shower and come to bed," Tate said. He gave her a last, quick kiss on the forehead and then released her. "In fact, I'll be lucky to stay awake long enough to crawl into our makeshift bed in the barn."

Perversely, Maggie felt a distinct twinge of disappointment.

Chapter Seven

Tate was already gone by the time Maggie awoke the next morning. True to his prediction last night, he'd been asleep when she finished her shower and made her way to their pallet. She had turned off the lantern and gingerly crept into bed beside him, leaving a discreet distance between them.

Then she had lain awake, silent and rigid, for hours.

She'd never known there could be so many annoying, disturbing, downright alarming sounds in the night. The barn creaked and groaned; there was an owl in the distance somewhere, and she didn't even want to think about what might be causing the other noises.

Desperate for sleep, she'd finally given up and inched closer to Tate...then closer and closer still, until she was touching him, huddling against his back, comforted by the reassuring presence of another warm body. But then, just when she was staring to relax, he had turned over...and had flung his arm across her, as well!

So there they were, facing each other, their bodies touching in so many places she couldn't begin to count them all, their heads only inches apart, so close she could feel his warm breath on her cheek. She'd barely been able to breathe at all. She hadn't known what to do.

But gradually—so slowly she didn't even recognize it at first—a strange thing happened. His arm across her no longer seemed heavy, but protective. His closeness was no longer intrusive, but comforting. A delicious warmth had spread through her entire body. She had sighed contentedly, then closed her eyes.

Maggie stretched and yawned, wondering if she and Tate had still been lying in each other's arms when he woke up this morning. And if so, what had he thought? Was he surprised? Put off? Turned on?

She got up and walked over to the barn door, surprised to see the sun so high in the sky. Then she remembered how dark the inside of the barn had seemed yesterday afternoon. It must always be that way. There was no telling how late it was...or how furious Granny Fortson was going to be with her.

Luckily, Maggie had slept in her jeans and T-shirt, so she only had to pull on her oversized sneakers before racing down the path to Granny's house. "Sorry I'm late," she announced breathlessly as she threw open the screen door to the kitchen.

"Hmmph!" the old lady snorted. She was standing at the sink and didn't turn around.

"I overslept," Maggie said.

"Your man was up and gone hours ago."

"He's not—" Maggie began, then stopped herself. "I'm really sorry."

"I don't hold breakfast for nobody."

"Of course not. I wouldn't expect you to. Where do you want me to get started working?"

"The day's half-gone already."

"So do you want to waste the rest of it criticizing me?" Maggie said, growing angry. "Or would you rather I did something useful instead?"

Granny turned around then, her eyes glinting. "Feisty little one, ain't you?"

Maggie shrugged.

"Your hair's a mess," the old lady said.

"I didn't take time to fix it." She also didn't have a proper comb—only the small one Tate had loaned her—but she wasn't about to go into that.

"Another few minutes won't make any difference at this late stage. Bathroom's that way," Granny said, gesturing toward a door. "There's a clean towel and washcloth, too. But don't make a mess."

Maggie was surprised by the old lady's offer. It seemed almost friendly. "Thank you," she said. She was even more grateful for the use of Granny's own bathroom, something she hadn't expected. "Thank you very much," she added sincerely.

When she returned to the kitchen, Maggie found another surprise awaiting her. Granny Fortson had put out a clean plate, coffee mug and eating utensils on the table. "Like I said, I don't hold breakfast. But the coffee's still hot. And the biscuits and sausage are probably still warm, if you have a mind to help yourself. I hate seeing anything go to waste."

"So do I," Maggie agreed, rushing to accept the offer before Granny Fortson changed her mind. "And thank you again."

After Maggie finished breakfast and finished washing the rest of the dishes, the two women went out to the garden to gather cucumbers. They worked apace for a while, but then Maggie noticed that the older woman was flagging. The heat was fierce.

She shouldn't be out here in this heat, Maggie thought, and tried to think of a reasonable excuse to get Granny Fortson back inside the house. She finally came up with one. "I wonder if being out here in the sun is bad for the cucumbers we've picked," she said.

Granny glanced at her, but didn't respond.

"I know it's my fault that we're so late in the day gathering them," Maggie continued. "But don't the ones on top of the basket look like they're shrinking up?"

"You trying to get out of work again?" Granny asked, narrowing her eyes.

"No!" Maggie said quickly. "What I was thinking was maybe I should carry the ones we've already picked back into the house. You could start rinsing them in cold water, and maybe even start slicing them, while I picked the rest." She waited a beat. "Of course, it's up to you. You know a whole lot more about making pickles than I do."

Granny thought about that, nodding while she thought. "I never picked cucumbers this late in the day before. They're probably shriveling all up inside. Won't make pickles fit to eat. We need to get 'em out of this heat!"

"You're right," Maggie said, gathering up a basket of cucumbers and heading for the house. "I couldn't agree more."

It took several more hours, and several tall glasses of ice water, but Maggie finally finished picking all the cucumbers. Before she went inside with the last load, she made a healthy inroad on the weeds threatening the garden, as well.

"It's a waste of time, spending so much of it picking weeds," Granny said when Maggie came into the house. "They just come back the next day, thicker than ever."

"I don't know about that," Maggie replied, holding up a plump eggplant. "Look what I found underneath all those weeds."

"Law! I clean forgot I planted them."

"I could make us an eggplant casserole for supper. If you don't mind, that is. My grandmother taught me her recipe."

Granny Fortson insisted on hearing the entire recipe, in detail, before finally giving approval to Maggie's suggestion. They had cereal with peaches and milk for lunch, and spent most of the afternoon washing and slicing cucumbers for pickles.

Supper was well under way, too, before Tate finally came in from the peach orchard. "You're late," Granny Fortson accused.

Maggie kept silent, feasting her eyes on him, thinking he looked better than anybody had a right to look. In spite of his black eye and scraggly beard, the image that came across was tall and tan, healthy and handsome.

"Who decides that?" he countered.

"Facts," Granny said. "The peach orchard closes down at six sharp, and it's a fifteen-minute walk from here. But it's almost seven afore you got home. What do you say to that?"

"I didn't walk," Tate replied easily. "I managed to hitch a ride and we went by the K-mart to get a few necessities Maggie and I both needed." He plopped a big plastic shopping bag onto the table. "Any more questions?"

"Money," Maggie whispered. "Where did you . . . ?"

Tate grinned at her. "It's day work. The Millers settle up with everybody at the end of every single day." He turned to Granny Fortson. "So nobody walks away from that place at six o'clock on the dot."

Granny dismissed him with a wave of her hand. "Lucky for you that Maggie here ain't a slacker like you are. She worked hard enough today to pay for keep for the both of you."

Maggie's mouth dropped open, but Granny had already gone back to the stove, busying herself there.

"I'll go out and get busy on the railing again, then." He winked at Maggie. "See you at suppertime."

IT WAS MUCH LATER that night when they were finally alone in the barn, that Maggie at last got to see what was inside the K-mart bag Tate had brought home. He turned the bag upside down and dumped its contents onto the blanket.

Maggie gasped, then eagerly rummaged through the treasures Tate had brought—shampoo, soap, toothpaste, toothbrushes, disposable razors, a large comb and hairbrush, a hand mirror, a new pair of sneakers that seemed the right size for her . . . and even new underwear for both of them.

"I take it these are for me," she said, holding up the lacy bras and bikini panties.

He nodded. "I had to guess at the size."

She looked at the label in one of the bras. "Good guess."

He shrugged. "What can I say?"

"I think we'd both better leave it at that."

"Good thinking," he agreed.

"Seriously, Tate, I don't know what to say, either. Except thank you." They were both sitting on the blanket, with the purchases spread out between them. Maggie got to her knees and leaned over to him, taking his head between both her hands. "Thank you," she said again, kissing his forehead. "Thank you, thank you, thank you," she repeated, kissing him again and again.

He fell back on the blanket, laughing, and pulled her down on top of him. "It doesn't take much to make you happy," he said.

"Not true," she said, laughing, too, as she kissed his bristly cheek again. "I'm very demanding."

Tate suddenly stopped laughing. He put his hand behind her neck, beneath her hair, and very deliberately guided her mouth down to his. He kissed her once, lightly, and once more the same way. Then he slanted his head and kissed her again, not at all lightly this time.

His mouth was hungry against hers, and his hands were moving up and down her back—soothing and caressing, arousing and stimulating at the same time. She was acutely conscious of their bodies touching in the most intimate of places, and of the hard, hot heat of him pressing against her thighs. She really shouldn't be doing this, she thought foggily. She should end it now, before things got out of control. And she would...soon.

She wasn't sure which one of them abruptly broke off their kiss. Probably, it was Tate. She'd been thinking she ought to, but hadn't had the willpower to do it.

"And what is it you demand, Maggie, in the way of a man?" he said huskily.

Somebody a lot like you, immediately flashed through her mind. But of course she couldn't say that. "Someone who's kind, thoughtful and generous," she said. "And sexy."

Damn! she thought. *I'm still describing him.*

"That's all?" he asked, lifting an eyebrow.

"And of course he'll have to think I'm the greatest thing since sliced bread," she added, trying to steer her way out of suddenly dangerous waters. "I'll be the most important thing in the world to him."

Tate stared at her for a long moment, his eyes searching hers. It was as if he could read all her secrets, and see into her soul.

"That's as it should be," he said at last. Maggie thought she detected a note of finality—and perhaps regret?—in his voice.

He kissed her lightly on the lips, then gently rolled to one side and eased himself away from her. "We'd better put all this stuff back in the bag and get some sleep. Workdays start early around here."

Maggie felt such a sharp sense of loss that it was almost a physical pain. She'd deliberately tried to extinguish the fire of sexual awareness that had ignited between them when they'd kissed. But had she done the right thing for both of them, or merely been a coward? She'd wanted to make love with him...and still did. And he'd wanted her, too. She'd felt the physical evidence of that while she was lying on top of him. Judging by that evidence, he'd wanted her very much.

Yet, she'd deliberately tried to put him off...and herself, as well. Why? They were both adults. Intelligent. Wise to the ways of the world. Why had she suddenly, perversely, thrown a figurative bucket of cold water on the idea of their making love?

It wasn't because she didn't care for him. Thinking about it some more, Maggie decided that Tate was all the things she'd been looking for in a man, without knowing it until she'd found him. He was caring and funny, smart and sexy. He had a goal in life, and a clear path he'd mapped out to attain that goal.

It was, she realized with sudden, blinding insight, because she was beginning to care for him too much.

And that scared her to death.

TIRED AS HE WAS after working at the orchard all day, then working on the farm after that, Tate was finding it hard to go to sleep. Impossible, so far. His body was tired, but wound so tightly with sexual tension that his muscles, including one in particular, wouldn't relax. His mind, which had been idling most of the day, was racing madly, crazily.

One thing stood out above all the others—for a moment there, he'd lost control, wanting so much to make love with Maggie that he'd willingly pushed aside all the reasons that he shouldn't. He'd been so caught up in lust that he'd temporarily abandoned all thought of his quest, and his dream.

Thanks to Maggie—and her remark about needing to be the most important thing in the world to the man she chose—he'd come to his senses in time. A narrow escape. For both of them.

He needed to be on his toes, alert and aware of *everything* going on around him in order to have a chance of succeeding at the nearly impossible task of regaining control of his company. Nothing—and nobody—could be more important to him than that. He couldn't let himself get distracted. And he wouldn't.

He had remembered to buy the Atlanta newspapers today, and had searched through them for any mention of his disappearance. He'd found nothing. But today was only Monday, still early for something to be in the papers.

He needed to get busy on pawning his watch. He hoped he'd be able to get enough money from the sale of the watch to buy transportation to take them to Panama City. Maybe he could find time to do it tomorrow. Granny Fortson would give him hell for being late again, but he was certain she was smart enough to know the monetary value of the work he'd already done for her. Not to mention all the work Maggie had done with the cucumbers for those damn pickles.

Maggie.

The thought of her had crept back into his mind. Again. Against his wishes. Maggie. The one with the smart mouth and unforgettable face. The one with the intelligent mind and sexy body. Maggie. The woman he'd always been looking for—without knowing it until he'd found her.

Maybe after all this was over . . . Maybe.

He sighed.

ON TUESDAY, Maggie picked, shucked and cut off corn for freezing; picked, strung, washed and put up green beans for freezing; and picked, washed and stewed tomatoes for canning. Granny Fortson supervised.

Tate came home late again, but this time he drove up in his own battered pickup truck.

"You steal that thing?" Granny asked in a steely voice.

"No way. I pawned my watch for it."

"Ain't no watch worth the price of a pickup."

"Mine was. It was worth a lot more than this particular pickup." He turned to Maggie. "I got taken. It needs a lot of work. But I had no choice."

She nodded her understanding.

"You going to work on the truck yourself?" Granny asked.

"That's right. But I'll do it on my own time. After supper."

"It'll be pitch-dark by then."

"I planned to use the lantern you loaned us."

Granny shook her head.

Tate exploded. "You'd begrudge us that? Why, you mean, miserly . . ."

"T'ain't that. The lantern wouldn't put out enough light for you to see. What you need is a proper mechanic's trouble light."

"I don't have one."

"I do. I'll go fetch it, along with an extension cord, so's you can rig it up afore dark."

Tate and Maggie watched the old lady disappear into the house. He sighed. "I suppose you think I should apologize."

She snickered. "I suppose it wouldn't hurt if you did."

He sighed again. "How did your day go?"

"Busy, but good. I really enjoyed it."

He raised an eyebrow.

"Seriously! Once you get to know her, Granny Fortson is an old sweetie under all that gruff exterior."

"I know," Tate said, holding up his hand in surrender. "She reminds you of your grandmother."

They both laughed. Then Maggie frowned. "How are you holding up, working two jobs dawn to dark?"

"I'm okay."

"I worry about you," she said, still frowning. "You didn't even take time to try out the new razors this morning. Or are you planning to grow a beard?"

He rubbed the three-day growth on his chin. It was still shaggy, but longer and thicker now, and much darker than the hair on his head. "I'm seriously considering it," he said slowly.

She stared at him, then her mouth formed a silent O as his meaning registered.

"I checked the Atlanta papers yesterday and again today, and there's no mention of my disappearance." He rubbed his chin again. "But a beard might not be a bad idea."

ON WEDNESDAY, Tate was late again coming home from the orchard. "What's your excuse this time?" Granny Fortson asked, turning around from the pot of cucumber pickles she was stirring on the stove.

"It's a really good one this time," Tate replied cheerfully.

"And what might that be?"

"I brought some treated pine lumber to replace the boards that have rotted away on your front porch," he announced triumphantly. Both Tate and Maggie had been chagrined the previous day when he'd finally cleared away the weeds to reveal the condition of the porch underneath.

Granny Fortson stopped stirring and carefully replaced the wooden spoon on the counter before finally turning around to face him. "I already told you," she said in slow, measured tones that held none of the delight Tate had expected. "I don't give charity, and I don't accept it."

Damnation, he thought. It wasn't as if he'd expected the old lady to do handsprings in appreciation of his offering, but a simple thank you wouldn't have been amiss, either. He glanced helplessly toward Maggie but she was no help at all. She had that damn frown on her face again. Her warning frown. Her please-go-easy-on-the-old-lady frown. He took a deep breath.

"It's not charity," Tate lied, fighting hard to control his temper. "The lumber was just lying out in the hot sun at the orchard." That much, at least, was true. "It would have gone to waste if I hadn't asked the Millers to let me take it off their hands." They'd let him take the lumber, all right, in exchange for a goodly portion of his hard-earned wages for the day.

Granny Fortson stared at Tate while he held his breath, wondering if she would accept his flimsy lie.

Finally, she nodded. "It's a mortal sin to let anything go to waste."

"I couldn't agree more," he said, breathing again.

"But I need to take a look at it," Granny said, heading for the door. "No telling what kind of trash lumber them Miller boys might try to foist off on an unsuspecting city slicker like you. And I tell you right now, I ain't having no trash lumber nailed to my porch!"

With effort, Tate bit off the short retort he might have made and silently followed the old lady outside. He was rewarded by Maggie's sudden appearance at his side. Latching on to his hand, she squeezed it and gave him the sweetest smile this side of heaven.

"You're a good man, Tate Rabun," she whispered.

And somehow, she made him feel it was true.

ON THURSDAY, news of Tate's disappearance made the Atlanta papers. Big time. Page one.

"'Prominent North Georgia businessman missing,'" Maggie said, reading from the paper. She looked at Tate, sitting beside her on the blanket in the barn. "You're prominent?"

He shrugged. He'd deliberately waited until they were alone in the barn, ready to retire for the night, before springing the news story on her. "They always exaggerate," he said, having read the account several times. "Most of the rest of it is general background."

Maggie held up her hand for silence and went back to reading the story. "The SCFC is a *multi-million-dollar* business?" she exclaimed.

"I told you it was successful."

"Sure. But not multi-million-dollar successful," she said accusingly.

He shrugged. She continued reading.

"Your disappearance was reported by your brother, Brian Rabun, and your mother, Elaine Rabun..." Maggie continued reading. *"She was in tears!"*

Somehow, Tate had known Maggie would pick up on that item. It had caught his attention, as well.

"I feel bad about that..."

"You *should* feel bad about that! Your poor mother..."

"But it can't be helped."

"Just imagine how she must feel! Her child, her son, missing and she doesn't know where he is, or what's happened to him, or whether he's alive or—"

"Maggie! I said I feel bad about it. Plenty bad. I don't need you trying to make me feel worse."

She shook her head. "I think you should get in touch with her, Tate."

"No."

"Just a quick phone call..."

"Tracing a phone call is the easiest thing in the world."

"Then maybe a letter, a little personal note...?"

"And where do you suggest we mail the letter? Where should it be postmarked? Here in Planters' Junction? Or perhaps in Panama City. Maybe we can include a return address, in case they have trouble tracking us down."

"You needn't be sarcastic."

"I'm trying to be realistic, Maggie. There's no safe way for me to get in touch with *anybody* without making my whereabouts known. The minute they find out where I am, you can bet they'll come after me and drag me back home to sign those merger papers. Is that what you'd have me do?"

"No. Of course not. But—"

"This is the only chance I get, Maggie. And don't forget one very important thing."

"What?"

He swallowed. "My mother was one of the people who betrayed me in the first place."

"Maybe she had a reason . . ."

"Maybe she did! But the best reason on earth doesn't change the fact that she did it! And I'm not going to deliberately throw all I've worked for down the drain now because of her. I know you think that makes me callous, but what other choice do I have? Nobody else is looking out for me—I have to look out for myself."

Maggie nodded and dropped her head. "I understand," she whispered. "And I shouldn't have said what I did."

The place was silent, except for an occasional creak from the old barn and the ragged sound of Tate's own rapid breathing. He saw a tremor go through Maggie's narrow shoulders.

Was she crying? Tate slowly and tentatively reached out his hand, putting his finger under her chin, then gently lifting it. She *was* crying. "Oh, damn, Maggie," he said, wrapping his arms around her, pulling her against his chest. "I'm so sorry. I didn't mean to make you cry." He stroked her back, and the back of her head. "I didn't want to hurt you. I never want to hurt you. Please, Maggie, please forgive me. You're my best friend."

"You're my best friend, too," she said, lifting her tear-streaked face. "And I just let you down. That's why I'm crying, Tate—not because you hurt me, but because I hurt you."

He managed a smile. "No permanent damage done."

"How can you say that? You've been hurt so much, by people you really care about, and now I've hurt you, too. And people will surely come after you now that they know you're missing. They could find you and take you away anytime. Tonight, even."

Listening to Maggie, Tate decided she was right about one thing. The police, and his family, could catch up with him at any moment; life and happiness were indeed fragile. Suddenly his reservations of a few days ago about making love with her seemed unimportant, irrelevant in the grand scheme of things.

"You're right," he said. He still had his arms around Maggie and now he tightened them, pulling her closer.

She looked at him questioningly.

"Life is uncertain," he said, kissing the tip of her nose. "And it's much too valuable to waste a single moment."

"Did I say that?" she whispered, sensing a difference in him, a new purpose, determination.

"Words to that effect," he murmured, lowering his mouth to hers.

For a brief moment, Maggie questioned what had happened to him, and was happening to her, to them. Then she closed her eyes, giving in to pleasure, willingly forgetting her questions.

He lifted his head to look at her and she saw that his eyes were dark now, darker than she'd ever seen them, and serious, filled with a fierce emotion that touched her, delighted her, ignited her.

She held her breath. Then he kissed her again and she lifted her arms to encircle his neck, her hands urging him to press his mouth harder against hers. She parted her lips and felt his tongue thrust inside her mouth, bold and strong, the same way he was, the way she was sure he would be. She tightened her arms around his neck, wanting to touch him with every part of her body, just as he had already touched every part of her soul.

Tate tried to hold back. He wanted to be gentle, to savor this moment, to make it last. But having Maggie in his arms as she was now—her passion meeting his, matching his—was pushing him almost beyond endurance. He pulled his mouth away from hers, trailing his lips along her cheek, down to her throat where he could feel her pulse pounding wildly.

He also felt her touching him, her hands cupping his face, then moving across his shoulders, along his arms and lower still, growing bolder. Her hands, slim and strong and seeking, were setting him on fire, igniting an almost desperate need in him. Letting out a low growl, he pushed her back onto the blanket, settling himself beside her.

"What was that noise?" she asked abruptly, her voice husky with emotion.

"It was me," he replied, his voice equally husky. "The male lion calling to the lioness."

"No, not that. Something else." She felt around underneath her and pulled out the newspaper she'd been reading.

"Oh," he said, taking the paper from her hand and casting it aside. "Nothing important."

"But it is important, Tate. They're looking for you..."

"Yes. But they won't find me tonight." He briefly touched his lips to hers. "It was just a night owl, so the only thing that's important is here and now, you and me."

After a moment's hesitation, she nodded. Their lips met, tongues touched, and the flame between them erupted again, burning hotter than before, almost out of control. Tate touched her breast, marveling at its perfection, feeling her hard nipple beneath the thin T-shirt and lacy bra she wore. He slid his other hand over the swell of her hips and stroked the twin mounds of her buttocks.

Maggie slipped her hand underneath his T-shirt, working her way up to his chest, stroking it, and finally finding a hard nipple to tease with her nimble fingers. Letting out a moan, Tate sat up and removed his T-shirt, then did the same to Maggie's. He released the catch on her bra and threw it in the general direction of their shirts.

He propped himself on one elbow to gaze at her breasts in the muted light of the single lantern. "Beautiful," he breathed after feasting his eyes on her for a long moment. He lightly touched the tips of her pink nipples with his work-callused fingers, then lowered his head to tease them with his tongue. Finally he buried his head between the softness of the twin mounds, pushing them against his cheeks with his hands, turning his head from side to side as he kissed one, then the other.

Moaning with exquisite pleasure, Maggie allowed her own hands to roam at will . . . caressing his broad shoulders, delighting in the muscles in his back, exulting in the sheer male strength of him . . . until her need was so powerful, she thought she'd explode.

"Tate," she said hoarsely. And again, "Tate."

"I know," he whispered, plunging his hand between them to unzip her jeans, then his. Quickly, almost frantically, they worked to remove the rest of their clothing. When they were finally naked, the desperate haste disappeared and they lay down on the blanket side by side, facing each other.

He touched her soft cheek with one rough finger and smiled. She touched his scraggly beard with one finger. And smiled, too.

He lightly ran his finger across her lips. She circled his ear with her finger, then rested her hand against his cheek. He turned his head to kiss her open palm, and his tongue darted out to tease it.

Then, without planning it, they moved toward each other at the same time, their arms encircling each other. Mouth met mouth, tongue touched tongue, legs intertwined, need met need, desire met desire, heart touched heart.

Without quite knowing how it happened, she found herself beneath him, her thighs spread apart, open and ready to receive him. Without quite knowing how it happened, he found himself poised between her legs... that hard, hot, pulsing, most intimate part of him barely touching that warm, soft, moist, most intimate heart of her.

He was breathing hard. His heart was pounding, and his mouth was dry. "Maggie...?"

She was breathing hard. She closed her eyes, then immediately opened them. "Yes," she whispered in answer to his question. "Oh, yes."

When he entered her, she felt a pleasure so exquisite that it made her cry out. Tate stopped. "Don't," she whispered, bringing up her legs to wind around his waist. "Please don't stop."

"I won't," he said, pulling back slightly before plunging himself inside her, deeper than before. "I couldn't," he added, burying himself in her welcoming warmth again and again, using slow measured strokes as he tried to prolong the pleasure.

He kissed her again, and she kissed him, clinging to him as they moved together in a rhythm as old as time and as timeless as love. Need grew along with passion, and Tate found himself moving faster, plunging deeper. Maggie was with him all the way, matching his every move.

Finally, the passion became something beyond them, an overwhelming force driving them further and further, beyond thought or reason, love or desire. Maggie felt it building in Tate...and in herself. She was as one with him, racing through the unexplored darkness with him, faster and still faster, until she finally was caught up in a wild rapture that shook her to the core of her being, then echoed and reechoed through her body.

AFTER THEIR LOVEMAKING, he held her in his arms and she cuddled her head against his chest, listening to the rapid beat of his heart, feeling his warmth wrapped around her. She smiled, pleased with him and with herself, totally content with the world. At least until the euphoria wears off, she amended, hoping that wouldn't happen for a long time.

"Damn!" Tate said only seconds later.

"What?" she asked.

"I didn't think to use any protection."

She hadn't thought of it, either. "It's a safe time of the month for me," she said, choosing her words with care. "If that's what you had in mind."

"It's exactly what I had in mind, Maggie—birth control. Nothing else." He kissed her.

She relaxed.

"I'll be sure to get a supply of condoms tomorrow."

She lifted her head again.

"Just to be on the safe side," he added. "In case something like what happened tonight happens again."

"You can count on it, Rabun."

He grinned and tightened his arms around her. Their lips met, his soft and silky in contrast to the scratchy beard surrounding them.

"We need to talk about leaving here," he said a bit later. "With the news of my disappearance already in the paper, I'd like to leave as soon as possible."

Maggie nodded. "When? Tomorrow?"

"I wish we could, but we wouldn't get very far in the pickup. It still needs more work. Maybe I can have it ready by Saturday. Or Sunday at the latest."

"Good. That'll give me time to paint Granny Fortson's front porch now that you've finished repairing it. And I'll be able to help with the rest of the canning, too.

Tate shook his head. "You're really a glutton for punishment, aren't you?"

"It's just that I feel sorry for her, Tate. She's really getting on in years. And living here by herself the way she is, all alone in the world, with no family to help her out..."

He guffawed.

"You ought to be ashamed of yourself, Tate Rabun!" Maggie said indignantly. "You'll be old yourself one day and—"

"That's not what I'm laughing about, Maggie. It was what you said about her being all alone in the world."

"What do you mean?"

"I learned all about Granny Fortson at the orchard. She has two daughters. One is married to Brice Miller, who owns about half the county, and the other is married to Tom Mooney, who owns the other half."

It took a minute for what Tate said to sink in. "Why, that old fraud!" Maggie said when it did.

"Exactly! She lives here alone because that's the way she likes it. She's independent as hell, and ornery as a mule."

Maggie started laughing along with Tate.

"Still think she reminds you of your grandmother?" he asked when he was able to catch his breath.

"More than ever."

Chapter Eight

They kept to the back roads on the drive to Panama City. It seemed like a good thing to do, since neither of them had a driver's license and Tate wasn't too comfortable about the handwritten title he carried on the truck, either.

Their farewell with Granny Fortson had been brief. "I don't hold no truck with gushiness," she said when Maggie tried to hug her. "It'll be good to have my own house to myself again." Even so, she'd given them a jar of cucumber pickles.

Tate and Maggie shared the driving. While he was at the wheel, she sang, tapping her fingers on the dashboard by way of accompaniment. She started with old, familiar songs, then slipped in one of her own.

"I never heard that one before," Tate said when she finished.

"Neither has anybody else. It's one I wrote myself."

"Really? No kidding?"

"Really no kidding."

"It's good, Maggie!"

"You're just saying that," she said, hoping it wasn't true.

"No! I really mean it. Have you composed any others?"

"A few." Tons. Most of them were junk, stuff she'd written years ago, but a couple she thought had potential.

"Do another one," he said. "One that you wrote."

She rummaged through her mind and came up with "A Hundred and One Ways to Pay Back the Man That Done You Wrong," a song she'd written not long after Royce got married. Tate whooped and hollered through the whole thing.

Then she sang, "Sittin' in a Stack of Bills and None of Them Mine," a little ditty she'd composed at work one day, when she was particularly bored with her accounting job.

"Fan-tastic!" Tate said, slapping the steering wheel when she finished. "Damn! I love those lyrics. They're funny as hell. And right on target."

Feeling inordinately pleased by his praise, she debated whether or not to sing the new song she'd secretly been working on during the past few days. She'd tentatively titled it, "I Was Looking for Love and Lost It, Then It Found Me." Tate might find the lyrics embarrassing if he knew he'd inspired them. But since he had no way of knowing, she sang the song, which was more intense and emotional than the others had been. After lingering over the last note, Maggie caught her breath and waited.

"Maggie, that's so good," Tate said after a moment, after an eternity. "So *damn* good! It's your best one yet."

She let out the breath she'd been holding. "I'll bet you say that to all the women who sing to you in your car."

"No," he said, shaking his head. "And I won't let you get away with blowing this off, either. You're good, Maggie. Really good."

He glanced at her. "What can I say?" she said.

"You can be serious for a change," he said.

"Okay, I'm serious," she said, making a long face.

"Sure. So why don't you use more of your own material in your act instead of imitating other people?"

She thought about lying to him, but decided on the truth instead. "It's too much of a gamble," she said. "If I fall on my face doing other people, that means the audience is lousy. If I fall on my face doing my own stuff, that's a different story."

The pickup truck chugged its noisy way along the flat asphalt highway. Maggie looked out the window and saw the distant stream of a jet plane heading north. Finally, Tate spoke.

"It's a gamble, all right," he said slowly. "I'd never have the nerve to perform in front of an audience of strangers in the first place. I admire you for being able to do it."

"But . . . ?" she prompted, waiting for him to drop the other shoe. He glanced at her and smiled, a boyish, one-sided grin that she found totally endearing.

"As long as you're in it up to your waist, why not go a step further, up to your neck? Or deeper. Hell, Maggie, you have the talent!"

"That's your opinion. And you're prejudiced. Or at least I hope you are."

"I am. But I'm telling the truth, too. And I really believe what I'm saying. So how about it? If my friend can offer you a singing job at his bar—or knows of an opening somewhere else—will you try singing your own songs, in your own voice?"

"That's a lot of ifs."

"Maybe. But like you said the other day, I have a really good feeling about this working out great for both of us."

Maggie wished she could share his optimism. Since they'd become lovers, she'd become a bundle of nerves. She wasn't sorry it had happened, in spite of the reservations she'd had beforehand. He was everything she could wish for in a lover, so that wasn't the problem.

The problem was that she no longer simply had herself to worry about; she worried about him, too. She cared for him. And the longer they were together, the more she cared for him. And the more she worried about him. She was disgusted with herself for being that way, but there it was.

She sighed. "I suppose I'll give it a try... singing my own songs. *If* this heap of junk gets us to Panama City, and *if* your friend can find a job for me and—"

"It'll work out," he said. "Trust me."

She sighed again. "Was there anything new in the papers this morning about your disappearance?" He'd bought an Atlanta paper at the gas station before they left town, but she hadn't read it yet.

He shook his head. "Just a rehash of the same old stuff. And I thought of one thing in our favor. The police must not have found my car yet, because there's been no mention of the Green Lantern."

She hadn't even thought about his car until that moment, which proved how inept she was at this sort of thing—being on the run and trying to evade pursuers. "I can't believe someone at the bar wouldn't have reported an abandoned car in the parking lot after all this time," she said after she'd mulled it over.

"They probably did," Tate said. "The next day or the day after that. It was probably towed away."

"But in that case, wouldn't the police know about it?"

He shook his head. "There are at least half a dozen holding compounds for lost, stolen or abandoned cars around Atlanta. I went to one of them with a friend whose car was stolen. You wouldn't believe the size of those mothers—they're huge, spread out over acres and acres, filled with cars of every size, shape, age and description."

Tate gave a short laugh. "There's no organized record-keeping. We almost didn't find my friend's car, even though we knew it was supposed to be in that particular compound. Somewhere. So you see, it could take months for the police to find my car. Or they might never find it. That's what I'm hoping."

"If that's the case, then how will you find the car yourself when you get back to Atlanta?"

He looked at her. "Maggie," he said slowly, "at this point, that's the last thing on earth I'm worried about."

THE BAR OWNED by Tate's friend was called B.J.'s on the Beach. It was the first thing they looked for when they got to Panama City, and it wasn't hard to find. It was smack-dab in the middle of the Miracle Strip, an almost solid array of hotels, bars and restaurants stretching out for several miles running east to west on both sides of Highway 98.

As its name implied, B.J.'s was on the beach side. A large parking lot paved in asphalt faced the highway. Beyond that was the bar itself, a rustic gray wooden structure with a huge window wall running the entire length of the building and offering a breathtaking view of the sparkling azure waters of the Gulf of Mexico.

"I'm impressed," Maggie said as she and Tate stepped inside the cavernous tavern.

"By the bar or by the air-conditioning?" he asked.

"Both," she replied. Even though B.J.'s was sparsely populated, this was only midafternoon and she wouldn't have expected many customers at such an off-hour. But the air-conditioning, turned down so low it almost made her shiver, was a welcome relief after the sweltering hours they'd spent in the truck.

"Let's have a beer and see if we can find my old buddy," he said, taking her elbow to guide her toward the bar.

They sat on stools and Tate ordered their beers. "Is B.J. around today?" he asked when the bartender returned with their order.

"You a friend of his?" the bartender asked in a suspicious tone.

Maggie didn't blame the man. With his eye still discolored from the brawl at the Green Lantern, and with the scraggliest beard she'd ever seen, Tate looked like a suspicious character. Not that she'd stack up much better than he did, she thought with a sinking feeling.

They'd both sweated in the truck for hours, with wind blowing in from the open windows their only source of relief. She'd tied her hair back with a ribbon, but was sure it was a wild, tangled mess by now. One look at her and B.J. Tanner would tell her to forget the farfetched notion of singing in his bar, or anyone else's.

"Yeah, I'm a friend of B.J.'s," Tate said, answering the bartender's question. "Is he here?"

"He's out back," the bartender said, moving away and pretending to rearrange things on the counter. "In the kitchen. He's pretty busy."

"He's not too busy to see me," Tate replied in a tone that caught the man's attention and made him turn around again. Tate leaned forward, staring the burly bartender down. "You can count on it."

Still the man hesitated. "Are you going to tell him I'm here or not?" Tate said.

"Who should I say wants to see him?"

"A friend. An old, old, *old* friend. Those exact words. Understand?"

The bartender eyed Tate for a couple of seconds longer, then turned around and left through a swinging door at one end of the bar.

"Tate, I'm worried," Maggie whispered as soon as the man was out of sight.

"About what?"

"The bartender. At first, I thought he was suspicious of us because we're so bedraggled. But then he became downright hostile. Do you suppose he recognized you?"

"How could he possibly recognize me? There's been no picture in the newspaper yet."

"Maybe your friend B.J. read the story in the papers and told the bartender he knew you."

"I suppose that's possible. But the man still wouldn't know what I look like. Relax, Maggie. You're being paranoid."

She was. She knew she was. She took a sip of her beer. "This is a nice place," she said, forcing herself to make small talk.

"It sure is. B.J. bought it a few years back with some of the loot he made playing football for the Atlanta Falcons before he got hurt."

She took another sip of her beer. "Doesn't it seem to you that the bartender has been gone a long time?"

"Maggie . . ."

"Well, for all we know, he could have called the police by now. They could come bursting through the door any minute."

The swinging door behind the bar was suddenly flung open. Maggie jumped.

"Old Hoss! I knew it was you!"

A giant of a man, so tall that the top of his head almost touched the doorsill, came into the room. "You son-of-a-gun!" the giant shouted, vaulting across the counter in a blur of motion, then enveloping Tate in a huge bear hug. "Where the hell you been all this time?"

The giant obviously was Tate's old, old, old friend B. J. Tanner. Feeling slightly sheepish because her fears had proved groundless—but also relieved for the same reason—Maggie watched the two men exchange macho ritual greetings.

Although Tate was tall, more than six feet, B.J. was almost a head taller. He was also quite a few pounds heavier, although Maggie felt sure his weight was in muscle, not fat. He had a huge neck and shoulders, and thighs as big around as her waist. His hair was black and curly, and he had a drooping kung-fu mustache. Clad in knee-length shorts, a Hawaiian shirt and sandals, B. J. Tanner made quite an impressive picture, Maggie decided. More importantly, he seemed genuinely fond of Tate—the kind of friend you could count on.

Tate finally reached out for Maggie's hand, pulling her to his side, then slipping his arm around her waist. "I want you two to meet each other."

"So tell me," B.J. said to Maggie after they'd been introduced. "What's your relationship with Old Hoss here?"

Caught totally by surprise, it took her a moment to find her voice. "We're traveling together," she finally said.

"More than that," Tate added, shooting her an accusing glance before turning his attention to B.J. "And don't you forget it, Tanner."

Well, Maggie thought. She probably should be annoyed by Tate's possessive attitude, but she wasn't. Not in the least. Quite the opposite, in fact. It was an effort to keep her grin to herself.

B.J. let out a long sigh. "Just my luck. Every time I meet a really great woman, she's already spoken for."

"What about your two ex-wives?" Tate asked.

"Both of them turned on me. Which proves my point—neither of them was really great in the first place."

Tate shook his head and grinned. "You never change, Tanner."

"Can't say the same thing about you," B.J. replied. "What's that god-awful mess on your face? You trying to grow a beard or something?"

Tate sobered immediately. "I need to talk to you about that, among other things."

"Sure," B.J. said. "Shall we sit at the table in the corner? Nobody'll bother us there."

Maggie was impressed that B.J. had picked up so quickly on the need for privacy. But she guessed that's what happened between friends who'd known each other a long, long time the way Tate and Tanner had.

AFTER TATE had finished telling B.J. the whole story of what was happening in his life and why he was on the run, leaving out only the details of how he and Maggie had met, he leaned back and waited for his friend's reaction.

"That's some bind you're in," B.J. said.

Tate nodded.

"But how did Maggie here come to be on the run with you?"

She laughed. "You might as well tell him that, too, Tate."

So he did, relieving the tension by giving them all a good laugh with the story of their misadventures ... from the Green Lantern to Mammy Yokum.

"I swear, Tate," B.J. said, wiping tears from his eyes, "I don't see how Maggie puts up with you the way she does." He shook his head and looked at her. "So you're a singer. Are you any good?"

She shrugged. "I think so. But it's hard to make comparisons when it's yourself you're judging."

B.J. stroked his kung-fu mustache. "I've been thinking about hiring a singer for this place a couple of nights a week. You interested?"

Maggie's eyes widened. "You can't be serious. You haven't even heard me sing."

"Honey, my customers would pay just to come in and look at you, even if you couldn't sing a note."

"But still ..."

"It's just a couple of nights a week. I already have a band on weekends. And it'll give you something to do while Tate goes out and gets the goods on the bad guys."

"I'll take it," she said, then turned to Tate. "I'm not like Granny Fortson."

He nodded, understanding her meaning—she *would* take charity when it was sorely needed and offered for the right reasons, as it was in this case.

"Okay," B.J. said. "You can start tomorrow night. You got something to wear?"

Tate started to protest, but Maggie evidently understood the question better than he did, and responded before he could.

"Yes," she said. "A black silk cocktail dress."

"Tight?" B.J. asked.

"I can't eat before I put it on."

B.J. grinned. "Perfect."

Tate wasn't sure he liked the direction this conversation was taking.

"Relax, buddy," B.J. said to him. "This is strictly business."

"I know that," Tate replied quickly, wondering whether he was that transparent or B.J. simply knew him so well.

"So that's settled," B.J. said. "Now we'll need to get you two unpacked and decked out in proper beach clothes. You'll be staying with me, of course."

"No," Tate said.

"The hell you say! Why wouldn't—"

"It's too dangerous."

"Come again?"

"If I'm tracked down as far as Panama City, your house is the first place my folks would tell the police to look for me. They know that you're the only person I know here."

"I hadn't thought of that," B.J. said, twisting his mustache.

"We'll stay at a motel. One that's not too fancy, and not directly on the beach."

"There's no reason for you to suffer," B.J. said. "I can let you have as much money as you need."

"We won't be suffering," Tate said, suppressing his laugh as he thought of the idea of sharing a lovely air-conditioned room, a completely private bath, and a soft, comfortable, real bed with Maggie. "And thanks for the offer, but we have a little money, and Maggie will soon be earning a lot more at B.J.'s on the Beach."

"Well—"

"The main thing I'm looking for is a clean, quiet, working-class motel, a place where we won't be noticed."

"Oh," B.J. said, slapping his forehead. "I should have thought of that." He glanced at Tate. "How'd you get so good at this cops-and-robbers thing so fast?"

"Necessity, old buddy," Tate said. "My entire future depends on it."

AFTER LOOKING around a bit, they registered at the Surf 'n Sand. Its main attraction—in addition to being clean, cheap and located a couple of blocks from the beach— was a king-sized bed. Tate and Maggie glanced at each other the instant they spied it, and immediately took the room. Tate paid in advance for a week, and registered them as George and Mary Todd.

"How on earth did you come up with those names?" Maggie asked as they deposited their earthly belongings—consisting of several paper and plastic bags—onto the counter and into the drawers of the vinyl mahogany dresser.

"Mismatched couples," Tate replied. "George Washington and Mary Todd Lincoln."

"An inspiration!" Maggie cried with delight, clapping her hands.

"And speaking of inspiration..." Tate said, reaching out to grab her around the waist, then pulling her toward the king-sized bed. She pretended to resist and he pulled harder, so hard they both lost their balance and fell onto the bed. Both of them were laughing.

"What an inspiration *this* is!" Maggie said, patting the bed.

"It'll take us to new heights of rapture tonight, me proud beauty," Tate said, wiggling his eyebrows.

"Or depths, as the case may be," she added, laughing harder.

"So be it."

Then they both stopped laughing at the same time. He touched her cheek. She touched his beard. "Here we are, in our very own room," he said.

"For the very first time."

"Yes. But not the last," he added, lowering his head to kiss her.

"Mmm," she said when he lifted his head again. "That was nice. Very nice."

"But?" he asked, reading her mind.

"I'll really be able to get into the spirit of things...you know, be inspired and all that...after I've had a nice soak in our very own bath."

"Spoilsport," he teased. "You wouldn't have made a very good pioneer woman."

"I'm glad I wasn't a pioneer woman. If I had been, I wouldn't be here with you right now, thinking about all the things I'm going to do to you..." She kissed him. "And all the things you're going to do to me..." She kissed him again. "And all the things we're going to do to each other..." She kissed him a third time. "After I've had a bath."

"I think I get the message," Tate said, chuckling as he got up from the bed. "And just to prove what a good sport I am, I'm going over to the beach to take a long walk while you enjoy the privacy of your very own bath."

"Don't be gone *too* long," she said as he headed for the door.

"I won't." He paused for a moment to blow her a kiss before he left, closing the door softly behind him.

Dear, wonderful man. Maggie stared at the door after Tate had left, then finally sighed and got up to head for the bathroom. She hadn't been kidding when she'd said she wanted a nice soak in her own bath. It was almost a desperate, yawning need by now. Granny Fortson had been kind in letting her use her bathroom, but the kindness hadn't extended to soaking baths or hot showers. For the past week, she'd only been able to take cold showers outside the barn.

Tate was right, Maggie thought, turning on the hot water and then adjusting its temperature. She was no pioneer woman. And she had told him the truth, too, she thought as she stepped into the lovely, warm, soothing blast of the shower stream. She had no desire to be a pioneer woman. She was perfectly happy to live in this lifetime—troubled as it was, but with all its creature comforts to compensate.

She planned to enjoy some of those creature comforts—a soothing shower now and a long soak in the tub later on tonight. Maybe she could coax Tate into joining her in the tub. She grinned and started singing as she elaborated on that thought in her mind's eye.

Feeling deliciously decadent when she emerged from the shower a long time later, Maggie dried herself with a white fluffy towel—nothing like the tissue-thin towels Granny had loaned them—then wrapped it around her body. She wound a second towel around her head like a turban. *Wasteful,* she could imagine Granny saying. Maggie giggled at the thought.

Stepping out of the bathroom, she was surprised to see Tate sitting in a chair by the window, reading a newspaper.

"Tate! I didn't know you were back."

"I heard you singing in the bath. I didn't want to disturb you."

"You wouldn't have..." She stopped, looking at him more closely. Something was wrong. Terribly wrong.

"What is it?" she asked anxiously. "What's happened?"

"Nothing much."

"What?"

He took a deep breath. "It seems I've been kidnapped."

Chapter Nine

"You've been *what?*" Maggie cried.

"Kidnapped," Tate said. "At least that's what it says here in the paper."

"But you told me this morning you'd read nothing new about your disappearance."

"I hadn't. But that was the Atlanta paper. This is the Albany paper." He got up and walked across the room, handing it to her. "It has a special section with news of the surrounding area, including Planters' Junction."

Her eyes widened. "Oh, dear." She sat down on the bed.

Tate sat down beside her. "It seems that somebody cleaning the rest rooms at the Midway Truck Stop in Planters' Junction found a bloodstained shirt and handkerchief."

"Yours?" she whispered.

"Yes. I dumped them in the garbage there. A stupid mistake on my part."

She reached over to touch his hand. "You can't think of everything."

He shook his head. "Maybe not, but I should have known better than to dump evidence in a public rest room."

Maggie frowned. "That happened a week ago. Why is it just now making the news?"

"Read for yourself." He pointed to a paragraph in the middle of the page.

"'Sheriff Cal Potts alertly sent the bloody articles to the state crime lab for examination,'" she read aloud. "'Results were returned late yesterday afternoon. According to the crime lab, many of the stains matched the blood of Tate Rabun, the prominent North Georgia businessman who was reported missing last week.

"'However, at least five additional blood samples, in addition to that identified as Mr. Rabun's, were found on the shirt and handkerchief.'"

Maggie stopped reading and took a deep breath. "*Five* other blood samples?"

"It was a good fight," Tate said. "I'd have thought there would be more than five."

Maggie started reading again. "'Sheriff Potts stated that the number of different blood types found on the handkerchief and shirt lends credence to the theory advanced by Atlanta police—that Mr. Rabun is the victim of foul play, possibly a kidnap attempt or...'" She stopped reading.

"Even murder," Tate said, finishing the sentence. "The Planters' Junction police are starting a full-scale investigation, which means they'll probably be calling the GBI and the FBI, as well."

Maggie shuddered. "And we only left there this morning. They were so close to finding us..."

"But they didn't," he said. *Not this time,* he thought.

"No, they didn't. Not this time," she whispered, voicing his fear.

They looked at each other. "Maggie—" he said.

"Tate—" she said at the same time. "You go first."

"I've been thinking. With all sorts of police coming into the picture now, crawling all over the place looking for me, things might get a little..." He hesitated, wondering how to phrase what needed to be said.

"Dangerous?"

"Oh, no. I wasn't thinking that." It was exactly what he'd been thinking—that some trigger-happy cop might be so eager that he'd get carried away, overreact, and that Maggie might be hurt, mistaken for a kidnapper. He couldn't, *wouldn't* allow that to happen.

"Like you said before, they came close to finding us today," he said. "It could happen again. I need to be ready to move fast..."

"Okay. We'll both move fast."

"At a moment's notice."

"I can do that, too."

"I might be forced to go into hiding until I can get the evidence I need. There's no telling what kind of life I might be forced to lead before this is over."

"Tate," she said in a small voice that didn't even sound like hers. "Are you trying to tell me that...that you don't want us to be together anymore?"

The look on her expressive face told him more than words possibly could have that he'd hurt her. And he didn't want to hurt her. Not Maggie of all people. But he had to let her go, for her own safety. Didn't he?

No! his heart screamed.

"No!" he said, pulling her into his arms and burying his face in the softness of her neck. "God, no," he repeated thickly. "I *do* want us to be together, Maggie. But I was trying to think of you... and the hardships you might face if you stayed with me..."

"I'm tough, Tate," she whispered, slipping her arms around his waist. "Don't you know that by now?"

"You don't know how rough this thing might get," he insisted, tightening his arms around her even as he protested.

"I can handle it. I'm not some fragile, precious thing."

No, she wasn't fragile. But she was precious, infinitely precious, and becoming more so every moment they were together. He was so close to being in love with her, he might have been there already.

She pulled a little away, leaning back in his arms to look at him. "You think too much," she added.

She took his head between both her hands. Her eyes, deep pools of darkest blue, gazed into his. Then she pulled his head closer, and closer still.

She kissed him. And he was lost.

He closed his eyes, breathing deeply of the clean, fresh fragrance of her. The essence of Maggie.

He increased the pressure of his mouth against hers, his chest against hers, to push her back into the softness of the big bed, bracing his arm to guide their descent. Then she was lying on her back and he was halfway on top of her, nestled between her thighs.

He stroked her bare leg, savoring its softness before moving his hand upward to her hip, slipping his fingers beneath her towel, then inching them across her smooth flesh until they found the mound of crisp, curly hair they sought. She let out an involuntary cry, which was smothered between their clasped lips.

He plunged his tongue inside her mouth, withdrew, then plunged again. His fingers found the warm, tender center of her, and he began duplicating the thrusts of his tongue with those of his fingers. Maggie moaned, tightening her leg around him while she moved from side to side, searching, seeking . . . faster, faster.

With a little cry, she flung her head back, convulsing again and again. Tate shuddered, as much caught up in the moment as she was . . . so much so that he was in imminent danger of explosion himself. He took a deep breath, then another.

Finally bringing himself under control, he kissed her bare shoulder, then put his head down next to hers, watching the pulse he could see in her neck, listening as her rapid breathing gradually slowed down. When it finally did, he closed his eyes. After a long time, she gave a deep sigh.

"Tate."

He opened one eye to look at her. She was smiling.

"Ah, Tate." She kissed his forehead. "That was wonderful. You were wonderful."

"I try."

"And you're modest, too."

"Always that."

She kissed him on the mouth, running her tongue along his lower lip and making him shiver. He felt her hand snake up inside his T-shirt, searching and finding his nipple, then teasing it until he shivered again.

"Maggie," he chided. "Are you trying to seduce me?"

"Yes," she answered immediately, pulling up his T-shirt. "Definitely." She lowered her head to his chest and traced the same nipple with her tongue. "How am I doing?"

"Great," he said with a laugh, shivering a third time. "And I'll show proper appreciation and response . . . as soon as I've had a shower."

"You can do that later." She reached for his T-shirt again, this time pulling it up to his shoulders. He lifted his arms and she tugged the shirt the rest of the way off, then tossed it aside.

"I should do it now," he protested mildly, enjoying her aggressiveness. "I'm all hot and sweaty..."

"Just the way I like you," she murmured, rolling over on top of him and losing her towel completely in the process. She grabbed the other towel wrapped around her hair and flung it aside, as well. "Just the way I want you," she added, lowering her lips to his, then plunging her tongue inside his mouth the same way he'd done to her a short time earlier. She lifted her mouth for a brief instant, just long enough to repeat, "I want you." Then she kissed him again, deeper than before.

With a low growl in the back of his throat, Tate surrendered himself to total pleasure—Maggie lying completely naked on top of him, her mouth hungrily plundering his, her soft breasts pressed against his hard chest, her bare buttocks neatly captured in the grasp of his two hands... He heard a low primal sound, and knew it came from some place deep inside him.

His jeans were constricting. Uncomfortably tight. He shifted his hips and Maggie, miraculously, understood and responded immediately. She got to her knees, placing one on each side of his hips, and leaned back. She unsnapped the top button of his jeans, then slowly, carefully, lowered the zipper. She looked at him and smiled— a smile that was sweet and erotic at the same time.

He was on fire with wanting her. His palms itched with the desire to touch her, and his tongue to taste her, and himself to bury himself so deeply inside her that they'd never be able to find him again.

But this was Maggie's show.

"I'm going to need a little help here," she said, hooking her fingers inside his shorts and jeans at the same time. He lifted his hips and she slid them down...

slowly...ever so carefully... He watched her face while she watched the slow process.

"My, my," she said when the jeans were finally over the bulge and down to his thighs. "Oh, my," she said again. He saw her tongue dart out to moisten her lips, and it was his turn to smile.

She glanced up and caught his smile. "Are you enjoying this?"

"So far."

"We've only just begun."

"I can't wait."

"I can see that."

She pulled the jeans the rest of the way off and tossed them aside with the rest of his clothes. Then she touched him.

He closed his eyes and clenched his teeth, but couldn't suppress the moan that escaped in spite of his best efforts.

"Do you like me to touch you?" she whispered, her face close beside his again, her warm breath caressing his cheek.

"No," he said hoarsely. "I hate it."

She chuckled softly and started doing erotic things to him with her hands, followed closely by her mouth. It was the most exquisite torture he'd ever felt in his life—such intense pleasure that it was painful. This time, he didn't even try to suppress his moans.

When he felt that he couldn't stand it any longer, he sat up. Maggie was still on her knees, straddling him, poised over him. He put his hands on her hips, holding her in place while he inched them both over to the edge of the bed, where his feet could touch the floor.

"My turn," he said, his voice so ragged it was a bare whisper.

She nodded.

Still holding her hips, he lifted his own and surged up inside her. They both cried out at the same time. Then she wrapped her arms around his neck, and he wrapped his around her waist, and they locked together hungrily, heedlessly, mindlessly, losing themselves in each other, driving each other relentlessly.

Time and again he plunged himself into her. Time and again she responded, meeting his thrusts with her own, urging him deeper, faster. Finally... after seconds, minutes, hours, an eternity... they reached the heights of passion and endurance almost simultaneously... then collapsed back onto the king-sized bed in a wild tangle of intertwined limbs and sweating bodies.

IT WAS MUCH LATER, after their rapid breathing and racing hearts had returned to normal... after they'd had a long soaky bath in the tub together and then made love again...after they'd showered together and then gone out for pizza that neither of them ate because they were thinking only of getting back to their room...and after they'd made love again and finally were sitting cross-legged on the tousled bed eating cold pizza...

After all that, Tate finally remembered that Maggie had intended to tell him something hours earlier.

"You expect me to remember something I started to say hours ago?" she asked incredulously. "After all this time and all the things you did to me?"

"Not to mention all the things you did to me."

She grinned. "Yes. That, too."

He reached over and wiped a dollop of pizza sauce from her chin with his finger, then cleaned the finger by sucking it. "We'd just been reading the Albany paper," he said, trying to stir her memory. "And talking about what a narrow escape we had from Planters' Junction."

"Now I remember! What I was thinking about, and was going to suggest, was that we need to come up with a secret code."

"A secret code?"

"Sure. In case the police start closing in on us. We can get a message to each other without anybody else knowing what it means."

"Maggie," he said with a laugh, "you've been reading too many spy stories."

"Just think about it. From now on, we won't be together all the time. I'll be singing at B.J.'s and you'll be doing . . . whatever it is you're going to do. Suppose the police come snooping around one or the other of us. Suppose one of us is in a bind and needs to let the other one know that there's danger without telling the whole world?"

Tate rubbed his beard. "You might have a point."

She nodded. "We'll need to set up a secret meeting place, too, in case we get separated."

"Yes," he agreed, getting into the spirit of Maggie's idea, which wasn't nearly as wild as he'd first thought. "Someplace that both of us can get to . . . dark and quiet."

"Or bright and noisy."

He lifted his eyebrows. "That could work, too. You're pretty good at this, Maggie."

"Thank you. And aren't you glad I persuaded you to let me stay with you?"

His muscles automatically tensed again. "I never wanted you to go, Maggie," he said slowly, as serious as he'd ever been in his life. "If I had my way . . ."

He stopped himself, leaving the words he wanted to say unsaid. He had no right to say them. Not now. Not yet.

He cleared his throat. "But there are no guarantees. If things get too rough, if I decide that you're in danger because of me, I'll send you away. Or leave you."

"Just like that?"

"No. Not at all like that. It might be the hardest thing I've ever had to do."

Might be? Hell, there was no question about it. It *would* be the hardest thing he'd ever done.

"But I'll do it," he said, watching her lively face go still, hating the world, including himself, for having to do this to her.

"But hey!" he said. "It'll probably never come to that. Maybe I'll get the evidence I need before anybody has a clue where we are."

"That's the other thing I wanted to ask you," she said, brightening a little. "What do you plan to do?"

"Well, actually, I'm not sure. I thought I'd go out to the processing plant tomorrow and look around. Survey the situation before I decide on a definite way to approach them."

"Couldn't you simply go in and confront them?"

"No, for two reasons. Number one, I don't want them to know who I am . . . and number two, I certainly don't want them to know who I am before I have a chance to find out all I can about them and their operation. So I'll have to approach them incognito."

"As George Todd?"

"Maybe. But that presents another problem. Not many plants would give a stranger access to their operation without his having a good reason for being there in the first place."

"So you have to gain access to the heart of the operation without them knowing who you really are."

He nodded. "It's a catch-22 situation. I thought I'd simply look around tomorrow and maybe come up with an idea."

"You'll come up with something. I'm sure of it."

Tate wished he could share her confidence in him. He was seriously beginning to doubt the wisdom of this whole escapade. But what other choice did he have? He certainly wasn't going to give up everything he'd worked for without a fight. He forced a smile. "And you'll wow those tourists tomorrow night with your performance at B.J.'s."

She made a face and put the last of her pizza crust back in the box. "I wish you hadn't mentioned that. I was trying not to think about it."

"Why? You've performed hundreds of times before."

"Not with my own material. Singing in my own voice."

"You'll be great," he said, getting out of bed with the pizza box. He carried it across the room, folded it and stuffed it into the trash can. "And I'll be right there, cheering you all the way."

"Do you think you should? I mean, won't it be dangerous for you? Not that I'm expecting a huge crowd or anything, but—"

"Don't worry," he said, stripping off the undershirt he had on and coming back to the bed clad only in boxer shorts. "You worry too much," he added, jumping in beside her. "And you wear too many clothes."

"Unlike some people I could name," she commented.

That sounded like a dare to Tate, so he responded accordingly, stripping off the man's oversized undershirt she wore, leaving her lusciously revealed in bikini panties—the scanty, lacy ones he'd had the good sense to buy for her.

"That's more like it," he said.

"I'll probably die of pneumonia in this air-conditioning."

"Then come on to bed," he said, patting the pillow beside him.

"Tate, we've both already been in bed. For hours."

"This time we'll get some sleep. And also talk about the secret code we should use," he added, knowing that would get her attention.

She scrambled up beside him and pulled a thin cover over both of them. Tate turned off the bedside lamp, plunging the room into almost total darkness, illuminated only by a sliver of light over by the wall where the drapes didn't quite cover the window at one end.

Tate wrapped his arms around her and she cuddled up close to his chest. They talked about secret codes for a while, but he quickly lost interest, distracted by the warm soft body he held in his arms. He started drawing little circles on her shoulder with his finger, then dropped his hand lower to trace tiny circles on the side of her breast.

"Tate?"

"Mmm?"

"I'm tired of talking about secret codes."

"You are?"

"Yes. Aren't you?"

"Wel-l-l . . . What else would you like to do?"

She kissed him.

He grinned and kissed her back.

Just another night in paradise.

WHERE WAS TATE?

Maggie swiveled around on her bar stool and glanced toward the door at B.J.'s on the Beach, for perhaps the twentieth time, then looked at her watch. It was almost nine-thirty, almost time for her show to start, and there was still no sign of him.

No message.

No phone call.

And most of all—no Tate.

Where could he be?

Taking a sip of her club soda, she tried to rationalize. They'd been running late the entire day. First they'd overslept. Then they'd lingered in the king-sized bed, taking up today where they'd left off last night.

She smiled at the memory . . . all the memories.

But she shouldn't be indulging in pleasant thoughts; she should be trying to figure out what could have happened to Tate to make him so late.

They'd gone out to breakfast, dropped her black dress off at a one-hour cleaners to get it ready for tonight and then gone shopping at a discount store while they waited. They'd bought beach clothes—bathing suits and loud shorts and shirts so they'd look like the tons of tourists who poured into Panama City during the summer.

And Tate had insisted on buying them matching watches, she remembered, smiling as she glanced at the one on her wrist. They were cheap but reliable, and Tate had adjusted them so they'd both always be operating on the same time. "Important in our line of work," he whispered, teasing her about her overcautiousness and the way she was turning into a regular Mata Hari. She only wished he would be *more* cautious.

They'd also bought sunglasses and tanning lotion, which was on the same aisle as hair care products, and she'd had the sudden inspiration of dyeing his hair darker. He'd agreed after only a moment's hesitation. So they'd paid for their purchases at the discount store, picked up her dress at the cleaners and then gone back to the motel, where she'd transformed Tate from a blond into a brunet.

It had been midafternoon by the time he finally dropped her off at the bar and then drove off by himself to investigate the chicken processing plant. Maggie looked at her watch again.

He'd had plenty of time to go out there, nose around as much as he wanted to and then get back to the beach. She glanced at the watch again. Yes, he'd had plenty of time, more than enough . . .

Unless something had happened to him.

She closed her eyes.

Please don't let that be true. Please let him be safe.

"Maggie?"

She opened her eyes.

And there he was.

"Tate," she breathed. She closed her eyes again, but only for a brief second this time before she opened them again. "Where have you been?"

He slid onto the stool beside her. "Working."

"What?" she asked, not sure if she'd heard him right.

"I don't blame you for being surprised. It was the last thing I expected, too."

"You actually got a job working at the processing plant?" she asked, getting excited as she thought about the possibilities. Tate would be able to find out everything that went on in that place!

"Not in the plant. All those jobs are highly skilled."

"But you'd know how to do them, what with your experience running the whole shebang back in Georgia."

"Not necessarily," he said with a grin, touching her cheek with the backs of his fingers. "And besides, all those jobs require a social security card . . . identification . . . references."

"Oh," she said, getting the picture. "And you wouldn't be able or willing to furnish any of those."

He nodded. "But the job I got is right next door to the processing plant. I'm hoping I'll be able to find a way to sneak inside at least long enough to talk to a couple of people and find out what's going on."

"What kind of job is it?"

"Construction. A new warehouse."

She frowned. "Do you know much about construction?"

"Not much."

"Then what will you be doing?"

He hesitated a moment. "Hauling bricks in a wheelbarrow from one place to another."

Her throat tightened. So much so that she could barely swallow. "Oh, Tate. Out in the hot sun? This humidity?"

"It's not so bad."

"You're not used to it," she said, wanting to cry for what he would be going through. "You could have a heatstroke."

"I'll be okay. I'm in pretty good shape. Especially after yesterday and last night and this morning." He grinned.

He was trying to make a joke of it, but Maggie was too concerned to go along with him. "Is it worth it?" she said softly. "Is it really worth all you'll be going through?"

"Yes," he replied emphatically, suddenly as serious as she was. "Every bit of it."

She took a deep breath. "What can I do to help?"

He took her hand, gazing directly into her eyes. "You just did it," he said, lifting her hand and kissing her palm. "Thank you, Maggie."

She swallowed the lump in her throat, and blinked back the tears that threatened to overflow.

"And an occasional body massage wouldn't go unappreciated," Tate added, reverting to his familiar teasing self.

Maggie managed a grin.

"Hey, you two! Break it up."

They turned around at the same time. B.J. was standing behind them, wearing knee-length shorts, a loud shirt and a wide smile on his face.

"It's showtime, Maggie," he said, placing his huge hand on her shoulder to give it a squeeze. "Are you ready?"

Chapter Ten

It seemed to Tate that he held his breath all the way through Maggie's first number. It was one he hadn't heard before, something about what it's like being in love with a football hero. He guessed that she'd had her old boyfriend in mind when she wrote it. Big deal. He couldn't help but feel a little jealous.

She accompanied herself on guitar, and B.J. had brought in a second guitarist to back her up. Tate reminded himself to thank his old friend for the show of support.

She seemed a little nervous, but Tate thought she was pretty good in spite of it. He had no way of knowing for sure, though, and also no way of knowing how the audience would react to her. That's why he held his breath a lot.

The room was about half-filled with sunburned and suntanned tourists dressed mostly in shorts and slacks. Tate guessed the audience was evenly divided between men and women, unlike the Green Lantern, where most of the customers were men.

When Maggie finished her first number, Tate applauded enthusiastically. He was disappointed that there was only a smattering of applause from the rest of the audience. Maggie glanced his way, catching his eye. She was definitely nervous.

He put on a big grin, and made a circle with his thumb and forefinger to show his approval. Then he put two fingers in his mouth and gave a loud whistle—the ultimate gesture of approval in a place like this.

It must have worked. Maggie shook her head, but she finally grinned, too. And she didn't seem quite as nervous when she launched into her second song, the hilarious little ditty he'd enjoyed so much when she'd sung it to him in the truck. It was about being totally bored with the job she used to have—being surrounded by a stack of bills, and none of them hers.

The song seemed to touch a chord with the audience, too. Quite a few of them laughed, and some of them even started clapping in time to the music. It made sense to Tate. They were here on vacation, having a good time, a lot of them trying to forget the boring jobs they had back home.

Tate crossed his fingers, praying the response would be more enthusiastic when Maggie finished her second song.

It was. And was he mistaken, or had several more customers wandered into the bar while she was singing? Either that, or the same customers were making more noise than they had been before. Either way, it was a good sign.

Tate breathed a sigh of relief and reached for his beer. He took only a small sip, determined not to repeat his outrageous behavior from the first—and last—time he'd seen Maggie perform on stage.

The applause when Maggie finished her third song was louder than ever. And she was visibly relaxing with each gesture of approval the audience gave her, getting into the spirit of the thing. She was giving back as much as she got, more than she got, which made the audience respond even more enthusiastically.

Tate didn't know much about show business, but even he could see what was happening between Maggie and her audience. They were responding to each other, feeding and exciting each other, falling in love with each other.

When she finished her first set more than an hour later—breathless but obviously elated—the crowd went completely bananas, yelling and screaming for more.

Tate yelled and screamed along with the rest of them... and was surprised when he suddenly realized there were tears in his eyes.

MAGGIE SAT with Tate at the bar during her intermission, but there was no chance for them to talk in private. People kept coming over to talk to her and congratulate her. A few even asked for her autograph. B.J. came over, too.

"Nice going, Maggie," he said. "Keep this up and I just might ask you to sing here every night."

"I warn you, I just might accept."

B.J. turned to Tate. "You didn't tell me she was as good as she is."

"You didn't ask me."

"What's the matter?" B.J. asked, grinning. "You jealous?"

"Jealous?" Tate repeated.

"Yeah. That Maggie here might score a big success and then up and leave you. Head out for Nashville."

"I've been to Nashville," Maggie said. "I couldn't even get a job as a waitress there."

B.J. frowned. "Did you have a good demo tape for auditions?"

"I had a tape. The sound quality and backup weren't too good, but they were all I could afford."

"What songs did you do?" B.J. asked. "Some of the ones you did here tonight?"

"No. I, uh, did imitations."

"Yeah?"

"Popular songs by famous people. You know, Dolly Parton, Reba McEntire . . . people like that."

"Maggie," B.J. said, shaking his head. *"Tsk."*

"They were pretty good imitations," she said, defending herself.

"So what? There are hundreds—no, make that thousands—of people who can do pretty good imitations. I know some people in the business in Nashville. What they're looking for is new talent, fresh material. Exactly the kind of stuff you did here tonight."

"Why, Mistuh Tannuh," Maggie said in an exaggerated southern accent. "You're enough to turn a poor girl's head."

"Leave this clod Rabun and stick with me, baby," B.J. said, wiggling his eyebrows. "I'll make you a star."

Maggie and B.J. both laughed. Tate didn't.

Too soon, it was time for Maggie's second show. Tate still hadn't had a chance to talk with her privately, which was probably just as well. He didn't want to say or do anything that would interrupt her concentration, or interfere with the mutual good feelings she'd built up with the audience. And the news he needed to tell her was almost certain to do just that.

"DO YOU REALLY THINK it went well, Tate? You're not just saying it to boost my ego?"

"I think it went better than well, Maggie. You were great! Terrific! The audience couldn't get enough of you."

"They could have been being polite..."

"Begging you back for encore after encore at the end of your final set the way they did? C'mon, Maggie. That's not being polite. That's *loving* you."

She leaned back against the headboard of the bed in their motel room and sighed. "They did seem to like me, didn't they? But not until after the first few numbers. I'll have to work on my opening."

Tate, lying beside her, smiled as he fought off the fatigue that threatened to overtake him. He'd worked long and hard in the hot sun this afternoon ... and had an entire day of the same kind of backbreaking labor facing him in the morning, only a few hours from now.

Even so, he was determined not to surrender to exhaustion. Maggie had worked long and hard, too. For years. And finally, tonight, she'd been a success. She was remembering that success in her mind's eye, recalling every moment of it, and he wanted to savor it with her. She deserved her moment of triumph, every bit of it, including someone with whom to share it.

He was happy to be that someone. And he wasn't going to spoil things for her by falling asleep now.

He also wasn't going to diminish her moment by telling her the bad news he'd learned today. He had to tell her sometime, but decided it could wait until tomorrow.

So he listened while Maggie talked—first about ways to improve her opening, then about all the grand things that had happened tonight. And when she finally wound down, they turned off the lights and went to sleep.

She was still asleep when he got up to go to work a few hours later. He was careful not to disturb her.

MAGGIE PACED the floor while she waited for Tate to return to the motel. If something had happened to him—if the police or someone else had tracked him down—she'd never forgive herself.

She glanced at the newspaper lying on the table, folded open to the story she'd read and reread at least a dozen times. She'd found the paper in Tate's dresser drawer this morning when she'd opened it to put his clean laundry inside after she'd walked back from the launderette.

She had guessed instinctively what was in the paper, and also that Tate had tried to hide it from her.

But why?

Weren't they in this together?

Since reading the story, she'd alternated between fear and fury—fear that he'd been captured and fury that he'd deliberately tried to keep her from knowing about the danger of his being captured.

Damn him!

"Damn you, Tate Rabun!" she said aloud.

He opened the door. Their gazes met. Locked. Neither of them spoke.

Finally, he glanced at the paper lying on the table where she'd deliberately left it so he couldn't fail to notice. "I see you read the paper," he said calmly.

"Damn you!" she said again. "You knew about this yesterday."

He nodded.

"And last night."

"Yes."

"Why didn't you tell me?"

He came inside the room, closing the door behind him. "There never seemed to be the right time. There were people all around us at B.J.'s bar."

"What about later, when the two of us were alone, right here in this room?"

"You'd had such a great night. I didn't want to spoil it for you."

"Didn't you think I'd be interested to know the police have been swarming all over Planters' Junction looking for us? Asking questions about us?"

"We both knew it was going to happen," he said. "We even discussed it."

"But not the direction it was going to take," she said, walking over and picking up the paper. "Not all the gory details. We didn't discuss the attendant at the truck stop giving a complete description of the two of us—*a highly accurate description* right down to what we were wearing."

Tate rubbed the back of his neck. "I'm not surprised that he remembered so much about you, but I didn't think he paid all that much attention to me."

If he was trying to distract her, it wasn't working. "We didn't discuss the attendant's remembering we were looking for a yard sale," she said. "Or that somebody would remember exactly what clothes we bought at the yard sale. And that somebody else would remember we asked directions to Miller's Peach Orchard."

"They seem to be pretty efficient, all right," he agreed.

"Be serious, will you?"

"Don't make it out to be worse than it is, Maggie."

"They've traced you all the way to the peach orchard! Isn't that serious enough?"

He crossed the room in a couple of long strides and clasped both her shoulders. "There's something you're not telling me, Maggie. What's really bothering you?"

"Oh, Tate," she said, tears forming in her eyes. "They know you're traveling with a woman. With me."

"So?"

"I wanted to help you. But now I'm a liability because now they're looking for a couple."

"Nobody at the peach orchard knew I was traveling with a woman. You never went near that place."

"But the paper said one man at the orchard remembered giving you a ride to Granny Fortson's place. They're sure to go talk to her and—"

"They already have," he said. "I read about it in today's paper."

Maggie caught her breath. "Oh, no."

She was totally surprised when he grinned.

"She met them with a shotgun. Told them to get off her place and not come back."

Maggie couldn't help it. She giggled. "They won't let her get away with it," she said, sobering immediately.

"No. But it buys us a little time. They'll have to get a search warrant."

"And after that . . ."

He shrugged.

"She knew everything about us, Tate, including our names."

"She doesn't know our last names."

"Even so—"

"And more importantly, she doesn't know where we were heading after we left her place."

"Maybe. But she's plenty smart. She could have figured it out."

He kissed her forehead. "You worry too much."

"And you don't worry enough."

"You do enough for both of us."

Maggie sighed. "I have to ask you again, Tate. And please tell the truth." She held up the paper she still had in her hand. "Why didn't you tell me about this last night?"

"Like I already said, you'd put on a great show at B.J.'s. The audience loved you. I didn't want to spoil it . . . at least not last night. I figured that particular news could hold until today. And that's the truth."

She wasn't sure she trusted him. "What if the police had moved faster than they have?" she asked. "What if they'd tracked us to this place last night, or today, while you were away?"

He hesitated, and she knew she'd hit a nerve.

"I thought about that—not about them finding us last night, but today while I was gone." He took a deep breath. "I didn't believe they'd harm you. It's me they're looking for. You're safe as long as you're not with me. And if they had found you today . . ."

He hesitated again. "I planned to search you down—find you—after all this was over."

His words hurt. He was being honest, painfully so. But at least he trusted her enough to be honest with her. And—truth to tell—wouldn't she have done exactly the same thing if she'd been in his place?

"I'm sorry," he whispered, not looking at her.

She took a deep breath. "Just don't let it happen again," she said huskily.

"What?" he asked, lifting his head.

"Don't try to keep important news from me—good or bad. Agreed?"

He looked at her solemnly for a long time, and she met his gaze unflinchingly. Something—she wasn't sure what it was—passed between them. A bond was forged.

"I agree," he said at last.

There was still something that needed to be said. Tate had brought up the idea of their splitting up some time ago and she had talked him out of it then. But things were different now. He would be safer now, too, if he wasn't with her.

"Tate," she began, gathering her courage. "With things heating up the way they are, do you think... I mean, don't you agree it might be a good idea if, uh..."

She couldn't bring herself to say the words. She saw the bewilderment on Tate's face, and saw it slowly change to understanding, regret and finally resignation.

"Are you saying you think we should get separate rooms, Maggie? At least for a while?"

"Yes," she conceded reluctantly. "I don't want to, but..."

"Neither do I. But I agree with you. It's the best thing to do right now. At least, I'll know you're out of danger."

And I'll know I'm not responsible if they find you before you finish doing what you came here to do, she thought. "And maybe I won't distract you with all my worrying," she said, trying to lighten the mood in spite of her aching heart. Tate smiled, but she noticed that the smile didn't reach his eyes.

"And it's not as if we won't see each other. I'll still come to B.J.'s to hear you sing."

"Somebody might recognize you..."

"It's not likely in that crowd. Everybody's looking at you. So everything's settled."

Maggie let out the breath she'd been holding. She took another deep breath and slowly exhaled it. "So tell me," she said. "How did your day go?"

Tate grinned. "I thought you'd never ask."

"Were you able to get into the processing plant?" she asked excitedly.

"No. But I thought of a plan to get inside it tomorrow."

"That's the best news I've heard all day. What is the plan?"

He frowned. "If I tell you, it'll just make you worry."

"I'll worry anyway, and I'd rather know. Besides, we have an agreement," she reminded him.

"Okay. Some of the workers at the plant go outside to smoke during their breaks. They gather under a big shade tree close to the site where I'm working. I plan to sidle over close to the tree during one of those breaks and then simply follow them back inside the plant."

She shook her head. "You'll be spotted in an instant. Somebody will know you don't work there."

"Not necessarily." He reached into his back pocket and pulled out a white mask, the type worn over the nose and mouth. "I bought this at the hardware store on the way home today. All the processing plant employees wear them. They take them off during break, of course, but put them back on when they start inside again."

"It might work..." she said. "But it sounds dangerous."

"Life is dangerous, Maggie," he said, kissing the tip of her nose. "Which is why you need to pack while I'm taking a shower. As soon as it's dark, we'll sneak out and go look for two rooms at another motel."

Maggie caught her breath. "Already? I thought..."

"We've been lucky so far, but we shouldn't press our luck."

She reluctantly nodded her agreement, depressed in spite of knowing they were doing the right thing. "We're paid up for a week here. Do you want me to ask for some of the money back while you're showering?"

"Definitely not. We're not checking out. As far as everybody else is concerned—except possibly B.J.—we're still staying at the Surf 'n Sand. Understand?"

She nodded again, swallowing around the lump in her throat. She hurriedly packed both her belongings and his while he was in the shower.

Later, Tate drove them to a motel well off the beach, but within easy walking distance of B.J.'s bar. "It's probably better if I don't try to drive you over," he explained.

"I'll be able to work on my tan while I walk," she said, trying to be cheerful.

He pressed some bills into her hand. "You register first. I'll wait a while before I do the same."

She couldn't be cheerful about that. "Tate—"

"It's just a precaution. I'll come over to your room to say good-night a little later."

"What . . . what name should I use?"

"Well, we could continue with presidents and their wives. How about Abigail Adams?"

Maggie thought a moment. "I sort of like Dolly Madison."

"Dolly it is, then."

They both tried to keep up a pretense of normality, but later that night after Tate had kissed her good-night and gone to his room, and she was finally settled in bed, everything caught up with her. All at once.

For the first time, she admitted to herself that she was in love with Tate Rabun. She loved him with all her heart, something she'd thought would never happen to her again. And with the admission of love, she also had to acknowledge her deepest fears for his safety and well-being, not to mention his entire future.

Anxiety bordering on panic settled in around her like a spider's web. She started shivering and couldn't stop.

She reminded herself of all the things Tate had told her earlier—how they might wind up on the run, moving from place to place at a moment's notice. She reminded herself that he'd warned her this kind of thing might happen.

But still she couldn't escape the idea that the web was tightening around them. Slowly at times, faster at others.

But inexorably tightening.

Chapter Eleven

Tate watched the half-dozen or so employees of the chicken processing plant from a distance, checking his watch frequently. He'd monitored their breaks carefully for the past couple of days and knew almost to the second when they would put out their cigarettes and start walking back to the plant.

He glanced at his watch again. Less than a minute to go. He wiped his sweaty palms on his jeans, wondering why he was so nervous. Probably the worst they'd do if they found him out would be to tell him to leave.

But there was always the outside chance they'd get really nasty and call the police.

He took a deep breath, checked his back pocket for the mask and slowly, casually, made his way toward the shade tree. He smiled grimly when he saw a man and a woman grind their cigarette butts underfoot and start walking back to the plant. One by one, the others followed suit. His calculations were right on target.

He picked up his own pace only slightly, keeping well behind the employees. Only when they reached the plant door and started to file inside did he start walking faster. He sprinted the last few yards, reaching the door right after it closed behind the woman who was last in line.

He reached into his pocket for the mask, pulled it into place and counted five. Then he opened the door.

The woman, in the process of donning her own mask, turned around to look at him. "Oh," she said. "I'm sorry. I didn't realize there was someone else behind me."

Tate shrugged. And held his breath.

After an eternity, which was probably only a bare second or two, the woman turned back around. Tate felt a gigantic surge of relief. The feeling was quickly replaced, however, by new panic when the woman removed a smock and shower cap from a hook on the wall and quickly put them on.

Tate cursed himself for not remembering the sanitary protection people in food processing plants were required to wear. Damn it! His own employees wore similar garments, yet he'd completely forgotten an important detail like that. He'd stand out like a sore thumb if he wasn't similarly dressed.

Then he noticed a couple of smocks and caps still hanging on the wall. All the employees he'd followed inside had left, heading in various directions, so the remaining outfits must either be extras or they belonged to people who were absent today. Tate reached for a set and slipped into it.

Feeling more confident, he looked around, trying to decide in which direction to go. *Eenie, meenie, miney, mo . . .* He settled on a wide corridor leading off to the left.

About halfway down the corridor, he came to the first of several doors on the right wall. Taking a deep breath, he touched the doorknob, turned it and opened the door only a fraction of an inch, leaning close to the opening to peer inside.

He saw a computer and a woman sitting at a desk.

Tate silently closed the door. This must be the administrative wing of the building, and all the rest of the doors probably opened on to offices, as well. He quickly turned around and retraced his steps, heading for the opposite corridor, figuring the actual processing operation—his primary interest right now—must lie in that direction.

Halfway down the corridor, he heard the familiar whirring sound of machinery. *Yes!* he thought with satisfaction. That had to be the sound of an assembly line operation. He hurried his step, heading for the closest door.

Again, he opened the door only a fraction of an inch, just enough for him to be able to peer inside. The room was big and brightly lit.

Inside it, people were processing chickens.

Tate opened the door wider, poked his head in and looked around. After a moment, he stepped inside and closed the door behind him.

He pressed himself against the wall, wishing he could make himself invisible and barring that, hoping nobody would notice him. At least, not until he'd had a good look at the inner workings of the plant owned by the consortium that was trying to assume control of the SCFC.

He scanned the room rapidly, his eyes focusing on details, his gaze missing nothing, his mind registering all of it and filing it away for future reference. He frowned in concentration.

"Hey, you!"

Tate was startled by the voice right beside him. He'd been so intent on watching the operation, he hadn't seen or heard the man approach. "Me?" he asked.

"Yeah, you. Do you see anybody else around?"

Tate's mind raced furiously. When he'd planned this break-in, he'd conjured up at least a hundred scenarios. But none of them had quite covered this particular situation.

He looked around, stalling for time. Then he shook his head.

"What are you doing here?" the man asked. "Why aren't you at your station?"

"I, uh, didn't feel well," Tate mumbled.

"If you're sick, you shouldn't even come in to work. You know that."

"I was okay this morning," Tate said, gaining confidence.

"Have you reported to sick bay?"

"I...uh...was just on my way there."

"I'll go with you."

The panic returned. Tate shook his head. "I can make it by myself."

"No problem." The man opened the door to the corridor.

Tate hesitated.

"C'mon. Let's go."

Tate had no choice except to follow.

The man closed the door behind them. "I heard there's a bug going around. You probably caught it."

Tate nodded.

"It's okay if you take your mask off out here. It might make you feel better...easier to breathe and all that."

"I'm okay," Tate mumbled.

"I'm not sure I recognize you. What's your name?"

"Madison," Tate mumbled, remembering the name Maggie had chosen last night at the motel.

"Madison? That doesn't ring a bell. You worked here long?"

"Not long."

"You'll like it," the man said. "The owner and manager, Mr. Garvey, is a prince of a guy."

They reached the crossroads and Tate automatically headed for the exit he'd come through a short time ago.

"Hey!" the man said, grabbing Tate's arm. "That's not the way to sick bay. It's down this way."

"I need to go home," Tate said, shaking free of the man's grasp and hurrying down the corridor.

"Wait!" the man yelled, running after him.

"Now!" Tate shouted, racing faster.

"But you need to punch out on the time clock."

"I quit!" Tate yelled over his shoulder, running as fast as he could.

He saw the exit ahead, but the man was gaining on him. Tate started peeling off clothing . . . the shower cap, the mask, the smock . . . casting them aside as he dashed for his life. With a final burst of speed, Tate reached the door.

He grabbed the doorknob and twisted it. It didn't budge. The man was close behind him, coming closer. Tate could hear the sound of heavy breathing. He could almost feel the man's hand reaching out to capture him, then hold him while they waited for the police.

He turned the knob again, and blessedly, mercifully, the door opened this time. Tate raced through to freedom, never pausing to look back to see if the man was still following him . . . at least, not until he was too exhausted to run any farther and finally was forced to stop.

When he did, leaning against a tree and panting like an animal run to ground, he lifted his head and looked around.

There was nobody in sight.

MAGGIE SPOTTED Tate the instant he came into the bar midway through her second show. He paused to give her a brief nod, then headed for a dark corner rather than taking his customary seat at the bar. Following the instructions he'd given her last night, she didn't acknowledge his greeting.

"'I was out there...'" she sang. "'No place to hide...'"

He'd told her it would be safer for both of them if most people didn't know they were together. She hated the idea, even if she could readily see the wisdom of it.

"'Feeling alone... all empty inside...'"

He'd also told her that he'd probably be late for the show tonight. She hated that, too, but was just glad he was here at last. She'd worried about him most of the day and night, even though she'd tried to put on a good show for B.J. and his customers.

"'Then there you came... you with your smile...'"

She wondered if Tate had noticed that there were many more customers here tonight than there had been before. B.J. had told her people had been asking him about her ever since she'd performed here the first time... wanting her back.

"'I hoped that you might stay a while...'"

Probably Tate hadn't paid any attention to the audience. He looked so tired—freshly scrubbed but still obviously exhausted. And no wonder! Tate was doing backbreaking labor all day, plus evading the police, and trying to find out everything he could about the processing plant. She wondered how *that* had gone today.

Maggie finished the song, then lowered her head, waiting for the applause. It came, loud and long. After a moment, she lifted her head, then her arms, and blew the audience a kiss.

She wondered what Tate thought of the new costume B.J. had furnished her. He had to have noticed that. She felt a little silly in it, but the customers seemed to love it.

TIRED AS HE WAS, Tate joined in the enthusiastic applause after Maggie finished her number. She was good—really good—and getting better with every performance. And that outfit she had on tonight was sensational. He wondered where it had come from. Probably B.J. It was exactly the kind of outrageous costume his old buddy would select.

On most women, it would have looked silly. Maggie made it look terrific.

It had a western look to it. Sort of. It was all black—black leotard top, black high-heeled boots, black leather chaps... and not just any chaps. They were cut out in front, and almost the entire back was missing, revealing Maggie's cute, pattable rear end encased in skintight black jeans.

The overall erotic effect was definitely planned and it definitely worked. Every man in the audience was very likely halfway in love with her. Or picturing himself in bed with her. Or both.

Tate was a little jealous, although not seriously so and figured that was perfectly normal considering how much he cared for Maggie. He trusted her enough to know she wasn't going to up and leave him to run off with another man.

What bothered him more was the charge B.J. had made the other day. He'd said that Tate was jealous because Maggie might leave him to go off and become a singing star. That hit closer to home. A lot closer.

Even so, it still wasn't true that Tate was jealous of her success. He was scared, not jealous... scared almost beyond belief that he might lose the only woman he'd ever truly loved.

It had taken him a while—sneaked up on him, actually—but he'd finally admitted it to himself. He was in love with Maggie Bennett. He wanted to spend the rest of his life with her, living life to the fullest the way she had a knack for doing but which had never come easily to him.

Not until he'd met her.

He'd told her once that he'd never had more fun in his life than he'd had with her. It was the truth. Every day, every hour, every moment with Maggie was an adventure—something to look forward to, something to enjoy... and then to think about and enjoy all over again after it was over.

She was the best thing that had ever happened to him in his entire life. She'd changed his whole world around, made him reexamine himself and his priorities. He owed her. Much more than he could ever repay.

And by damn, he certainly wouldn't dishonor all she'd given him by being so petty as to stand in the way of her success!

He'd be with her all the way—backing her up, encouraging her, doing everything he could do to send her to Nashville or wherever she wanted to go with all the enthusiasm he could muster.

Even if it broke his heart.

Which it very well might do.

AFTER MAGGIE finished her last show, she changed into shorts and a T-shirt. Then she and Tate took off their shoes and went for a walk on the beach. She left her costume at the bar as Tate suggested.

"It'll probably be easier if you leave your work clothes at the bar all the time," he said. "Especially since you'll be singing every night now." He draped his arm around her shoulders and gave her a squeeze. "Congratulations."

"You don't mind?"

"Mind? Hell, I'm proud of you! B.J. might have taken you on as a favor to me, but he'd never offer you a job singing every night if you weren't bringing in customers."

"You wouldn't kid a kidder, would you?"

"Not about something like this. Trust me. With B.J., the bottom line is everything. You have to be bringing in big bucks for him. Why else would he buy you that new costume?"

"Ah, yes," she said. "The new costume. I felt a little silly in it. What did you think, Tate? Honestly."

"About what every other man in the room thought, I imagine. That I'd like to be the one to peel it off of you."

"Jealous?" she asked, sounding pleased.

"Damn right," Tate said. "Especially because I didn't get to do it tonight."

"But enough about that," she said. "I'm dying to hear what you found out at the processing plant today."

"One thing I found out is that I shouldn't give up my day job and try for a career in the secret service. I'd never make it as a spy."

"Oh?" Maggie said, lifting an eyebrow.

Tate told her about his bungled attempt to uncover secrets at the processing plant, sparing himself nothing, finishing up with his wild striptease as he raced down the corridor at the plant while trying to elude his pursuer. It hadn't been funny to him at the time—far from it—but when he finished telling the story, he was laughing as hard as Maggie was.

"And that's it?" she asked when she finally stopped laughing.

"Well, actually, I managed to find out a couple of things in spite of myself," Tate said. "For one, the plant itself is clean enough but the equipment is so outmoded, it looks as if it could have come off Noah's ark. I was amazed that they're still using machinery and methods that most people discarded years ago."

Maggie stopped walking. "That's wonderful, Tate! For you, I mean. Isn't that enough to discredit the consortium?"

"Not really," he said, rubbing the back of his neck. "Not by itself. They claimed to have a fully operational plant here. It is that, although how long it can keep operating without a major overhaul is anybody's guess."

"But if you told your board of directors what you've found here..."

"They might have second thoughts about the merger. Or they might not. I don't trust them. That's why I'd like to have something more concrete to hit them with when I go back."

"Surely you don't plan to sneak into the processing plant again!" Maggie exclaimed.

"Not anytime soon, that's for sure. But I did find out one other thing today that might be a possible lead. I thought I might ask you to help me follow up on it."

"Me?" she asked excitedly. "Yes! I'll do it."

He laughed. "You don't even know what it is, yet."

"I'll do it anyway. Tell me what it is."

"Well... before he started chasing me, the guy who questioned me inside the plant today mentioned something. He said the place was owned and managed by a Mr. Garvey."

"And . . . ?"

"The financial consortium told us that *they* owned the plant. They never mentioned a Mr. Garvey . . ." Tate deliberately paused a moment for effect. "And nobody by that name is a member of the consortium," he added.

"Oh," Maggie said. Then she repeated, "Oh."

"Exactly. So I thought maybe you could phone the plant tomorrow, pretending to be a reporter researching a story, and find out what you can about this Mr. Garvey."

"Excellent!" Maggie said. "But better still, why don't I go out there in person?"

Tate shook his head. "Too dangerous."

"But—"

"And also not necessary. For our purposes, you can find out everything we need to know by telephone—his full name, and whether he actually does or does not own the company. If it's possible, you might even talk to him over the phone."

"I could set up an appointment for an interview."

Tate thought for a moment, then nodded. "That's okay. If it's fully understood—by you—that you'll never keep that appointment."

"Tate—"

"I mean it, Maggie. Another false move by either of us at this point could destroy everything I've been trying to do."

Tate looked at her beautiful face, illuminated not only by the moon and stars, but also by dozens of neon lights along the shore. He saw her disappointment, and hated himself for causing it. But he could deal with that.

What he couldn't deal with was the idea of deliberately putting her in danger, which he might be doing if he allowed her to go out to the processing plant in person.

He took a deep breath. "Will you do it, Maggie, my way? Will you help me?"

"You know I will."

He kissed his own finger, then touched the finger to her nose. "Thank you."

She sighed. "We'll need to go over what I need to say."

"We will. Later." This time, he pulled her into his arms. He tilted her chin up with his finger and kissed her. He'd been wanting to do that for hours.

This time, he was the one who sighed when they broke apart. "I read some more news in the afternoon papers," he said. "Good news this time. The police got their search warrant and went back to Granny Fortson's house."

"You call that good news?"

Tate chuckled. "She told them all about us."

"That's terrible! And why are you laughing?"

"She told them that out of the goodness of her heart, she let a couple—brother and sister—stay at her place for about a week."

"Surely she didn't say that!" Maggie exclaimed, her mouth dropping open.

"Oh, but she did. She said the man worked at the peach orchard to earn a few pennies—very few—while she nursed his little sister back to health."

"Oh, good grief!" Maggie said, starting to laugh.

"It seems that you were malnourished, probably suffering from scurvy, according to Granny. But she put you to rights again. Fixed you up just fine before she finally allowed you to get out of bed and go on your way again."

"What an imagination!"

"Yep. Granny told the police she thought we were Puerto Rican or German—some kind of foreigners, at least. And she thought we were headed for either the California or Texas border. She wasn't sure which."

"That old fraud!"

"Yeah. Granny's been up to her old tricks, all right."

"Thank God for Granny."

"I agree," Tate said, draping his arm around Maggie's shoulders. They started walking again. "She certainly did everything in her power to throw the police off our trail."

Maggie stopped again. "That's it!"

"What?"

"We'll use Granny for our secret code. We never did decide on one, remember?"

"I remember. But we should be able to relax a little now and not worry about such things."

Maggie shook her head. "The police aren't stupid, Tate. They aren't going to drop their entire investigation because of an old woman's blatant lies."

Tate knew that. But he'd hoped Maggie didn't. She worried too much, and he'd tried to ease her fears, at least for a short time. He sighed. "You're right. So how do you suggest we use Granny Fortson as our secret code?"

"We'll keep it as simple as possible. *Granny* will be our key word and anything we say after that will describe the situation. For instance, I could tell you, 'Granny's sick, but the doctors said not to worry.' And that would mean there's danger, but it's not too serious."

"That's good," Tate said, nodding his agreement. "And something like 'Granny's close to death,' would mean there's real danger, and we should meet at our secret place."

"Exactly! And speaking of our secret meeting place..."

"I know," he said, holding up his hands. "We never did decide on one. Do you want to look for a place now?"

"Here on the beach?" she said, glancing around. "Everything is so open, exposed. There's no place to hide."

"That's true down close to the water, but it's not a problem only a few yards inland." He pointed to the dark shadows surrounding a beachfront motel some yards from the ocean.

"I'm not sure," she said, still unconvinced. "But I suppose we could at least take a look."

After much searching, discarding and a couple of heated arguments, they decided on a spot. It was directly on the beach, close to the water, at one end of a large cabana beside the pool of a high-rise condo. They figured they could use it as a meeting place either in daytime or at night.

"It's getting late," Maggie said when they finally reached an agreement. "Shouldn't we start walking back to B.J.'s to get the truck?"

Tate shook his head.

"No?"

"I decided we should celebrate Granny's inspired tall tales," he said. "So I rented you a suite on the beach for tonight."

"A suite?" she repeated.

"It's not all that fancy," he said with a laugh. "But it does have a separate living room and a wet bar with a refrigerator. And I remembered to put a bottle of champagne in the refrigerator."

Maggie raised her eyebrows. "You've changed your mind about our needing to have separate rooms?"

"No," he said slowly, wondering if this had been such a good idea after all. "I have a room at another motel a couple of blocks away."

"So now we have separate motels," she said in a fractured little voice that almost broke his heart.

Stupid, stupid, stupid. "Only for tonight," he said, cursing himself for the fool he was. "I decided you deserved a little luxury after all the places we've been staying."

"I see," she said in that same little voice.

"Dammit, Maggie! I wanted to do something nice for you. What's wrong with that?"

"Nothing. Really. And I appreciate the thought."

"But . . . ?"

"I'd rather be with you. I mean, at least nearby."

Tate clenched his fists, took a deep breath and wrapped his arms around her narrow shoulders. He pulled her close, loving the feel of her and the way her body fit against his. Perfectly. As if they were made for each other.

"I'd rather be with you, too," he said, kissing the top of her head. "It was a lousy idea."

"But a generous gesture and—"

"Maggie," he said, placing his finger against her lips to silence her. "There'll be no more separate motels. I promise."

Chapter Twelve

Tate watched Maggie as she dialed the telephone number he'd written down for her. Having a private phone in the room was a fringe benefit of the suite he'd splurged on renting for her. About the only one, as far as he could tell. He'd left her almost in tears last night, and then gone to his own lonely motel room for a miserable, sleepless night. It hadn't helped his mood to find her looking almost as bad as he felt this morning.

"Hullo," Maggie said after a moment, speaking with a cultured English accent that would have fooled Tate himself if he hadn't known better. "Hillary Monroe here, from Channel Eleven News. Would you be so kind as to ring Mr. Garvey's secretary for me? Oh, and I'm afraid I've misplaced my notes with the secretary's name... Could you give me that, too, please?"

Maggie paused, pencil in hand. "Ms. Ashton?" she said, writing it down. "Thank you very much."

After much discussion, Tate and Maggie had decided she should pretend to work for a television station rather than a newspaper. They'd chosen her name by keeping to their policy of using and sometimes mixing presidents and their wives. The English accent was strictly Maggie's idea.

"Ms. Ashton?" Maggie said after a moment. "Hillary Monroe here, from Channel Eleven News. But I imagine you were expecting my call." Another pause. "No? Our public relations people were supposed to contact you. I'm sure you'll be hearing from them later.

"In the meantime, I wonder if you might give me a little background information. It's for the feature story we're doing on Mr. Garvey."

Tate watched Maggie, seeing her face register surprise, then indignation at whatever it was Ms. Ashton was saying.

"You've never heard of such a story and never heard of me, either? Well, as I told you, our public relations people have been terribly remiss. I was under the impression that Mr. Garvey had already agreed to be interviewed."

Maggie laughed. "As for never having heard of me, I don't doubt it for a moment. I'm not an on-camera personality. I'm a producer—the person who makes decisions about who you *will* see on the air."

She listened, nodding this time. "That's quite all right, Ms. Ashton. I understand you're merely doing your job, as a proper secretary would do. It's quite commendable." She listened again, winking at Tate.

"Yes, I quite understand. And I'll be brief. I merely need to verify some information.

"First of all, would you give me the correct spelling of Mr. Garvey's name, please?" She nodded and repeated the letters while she wrote his name. "L-l-o-y-d. Lloyd Garvey. That's what we had, but I wanted to be certain.

"Right. Now. As I understand it, Mr. Garvey is both the owner and manager of the processing plant. Is that correct?"

Maggie listened, then nodded. "Correct. And I was also under the impression that there's a second processing plant in Birmingham, Alabama. Does Mr. Garvey own that plant, as well?"

Again, she listened to Ms. Ashton on the phone. "Oh, I see. The Birmingham plant is owned by Mr. Garvey's brother, Floyd Garvey."

Maggie listened some more, then took a deep breath. "In that case, Ms. Ashton, could you tell me something? Exactly what relationship do both Mr. Garvey and his brother have with Midsouth Investment Company?"

Maggie waited.

And Tate waited, holding his breath.

"Who am I?" Maggie said after a moment. "I already told you. And I also explained that... What? Of course not! Wait..."

Maggie held the receiver away from her head and looked at it. Then she looked at Tate. "She hung up."

"So I gathered," he said.

"She was a bit huffy, too, I might add."

"I suppose it was your mention of the financial consortium that set her off."

"You might say that, yes. Ms. Ashton has very strong—very negative—feelings about Midsouth Investment Company. What's going on, Tate?"

"I only wish I knew."

"That was a good guess you had—about this plant being closely connected to the Birmingham plant in some way. Mr. Garvey's brother owns the other one."

"Don't give me credit. It was Midsouth that claimed to own both plants. I was merely checking on their claim."

"Is that the proof you need to go back to your board of directors?" Maggie asked.

"Almost. We're certainly on the right track."

"What else do you need?"

He took a deep breath. "I'm going to have to try to talk to Mr. Lloyd Garvey in person."

"Oh, no."

"Not right this minute," he said reassuringly. "First, we have to come up with a plan better than the harebrained scheme I had last time. I need some reason, a logical and reasonable one, to get inside that plant. Then I need to find out what Garvey's relationship is with Midsouth. Preferably before he throws me out or calls the cops."

"Isn't that the same predicament you were in before—the catch-22 situation?"

"It's not quite the same. Now we know that Garvey's personal secretary strongly dislikes the consortium for some reason. And if I can just find out what that reason is, I won't mind it if Garvey calls the cops on me. I'll have done all I can do to discredit Midsouth by that time, so I'll be ready to go home."

"Oh."

Seeing Maggie's distress, Tate quickly tried to reassure her. "Don't worry. Just because I'll be leaving doesn't mean that you have to do the same. You're not a fugitive."

He took her hand. It was cold, so he held it between both of his. "You're a big success here, Maggie. I wouldn't be selfish enough to ask you to give it up."

He wanted to ask her to do exactly that . . . to chuck everything she'd worked for and come away with him. But he wouldn't.

"Besides," he said. "Panama City is only a few hours from Atlanta, if you don't detour by way of Granny Fortson's. I'll be back to see you."

"You promise?" Her voice was choked.

"Count on it," he said, kissing the palm of her hand, then folding her fingers to hold the kiss inside. "I'll be here so often, you probably won't even know I've been gone."

She lifted her other hand to touch his cheek, then stroke his beard. "I'll know you've been gone, Tate," she said.

His throat tightened at her simple, softly spoken words. "But I'm not gone yet. And I won't be gone anytime soon unless we can come up with a good plan to get me inside that plant."

"We'll think of something."

"Sure," he agreed. "The two of us together are unbeatable. But we'll think better after some breakfast. Why don't you call room service and order us the works?"

"What about your job? Aren't you supposed to work today?"

"I already told them I'd be late. I wanted to be here while you called Lloyd Garvey. Another few minutes won't make any difference. Besides . . ." He touched her hand, which still rested against his cheek. "I missed you last night."

He didn't voice the thought that was uppermost in his mind, but her look told him clearer than words that she already knew. Each time they were together might be their last, at least for a long, long time. With things as unsettled as they were—his upcoming confrontation with his brother, mother and the SCFC board of directors back in Atlanta, and Maggie's own success that might take her anywhere—every moment was precious.

"I missed you, too." Her forced smile was sweet, brave and sad at the same time.

Tate cleared his throat. "And after breakfast, I want you to promise me that you'll relax and have some fun for a change."

"Relax and have fun?" she repeated. "At a time like this?"

"I can't think of a better one." He squinted one eye while he took a closer look at her. "You're so pale, nobody would even know you've been to the beach."

"That's what comes with hanging out in bars all the time. You never get a suntan."

"We'll change that today. And to show you what a sport I am, I'll even rub lotion on your back before I leave for work."

"You're too good to me."

"I know," he said, reaching out to her, pulling her close and smiling as he lightly touched his lips to hers. "And you're too good to me."

"I'LL SHOW YOU something if you'll promise you won't hit me up for too big a raise," B.J. said.

Maggie looked up from the crossword puzzle she'd been working. The late-afternoon sun filtered into the bar through lowered blinds behind the corner table where she was sitting. Later tonight—if past nights were an indication—B.J.'s on the Beach would be packed to overflowing, but for now it was nearly deserted.

At this time of day, the bar was cool and quiet, a much more comfortable place to pass time in than a claustrophobic motel room. After returning from the beach today, she'd tried to sleep but she kept thinking of Tate, missing him terribly. Then she'd felt as if the walls were closing in on her, so she got up and came to the bar.

"How much do you think I should ask for?" she asked B.J. He was standing beside her, towering over the table with a broad grin on his face. She had no intention of asking for any kind of raise. B.J. had already been more than generous to her and Tate, and she considered him a real friend to both of them.

"Read it first," B.J. said, shoving the entertainment page of the local paper in front of her.

Maggie glanced at the paper, then back to B.J. "Local sensation?" she said. "New queen of the Miracle Strip?"

"There's more," he said. "Read on."

" 'Maggie Bennett,' " she said, reading from the paper, " 'continues to wow the customers at B.J.'s on the Beach, bringing in new fans every night. If you haven't visited Panama City's longtime favorite watering hole recently, do it now! Right this minute, while you can catch the lovely, charming, talented Maggie B. She's the hottest thing to hit this town since the heat wave of 1988.' "

"Well?" B.J. asked.

Maggie blinked. "My goodness."

"Not bad, huh?"

"I—I'm flabbergasted."

"Maggie, honey," B.J. said, pulling out a chair and sitting down beside her. "You know you're good. I've already told you that."

"I thought you were exaggerating. You know, being a friend and all."

"I'd never lie to a friend. Especially about something like this," B.J. said, totally serious for one of the few times since she'd met him. "This is the real thing, Maggie," he added, pointing to the newspaper. "Your fans. Your success. Your rave review."

B.J. hesitated. "The question is, where do you go from here?"

"I'm not sure," she said, deliberately choosing to misinterpret his meaning. "Tate's situation is still up in the air, so there's no way of knowing—"

"Maggie," he interrupted, shaking his head. "We're not talking about you and Tate here and you know it. We're talking about *you*, and what you intend doing with your career. Your relationship with Tate and your plans for your career are not one and the same. But you know that, too."

She did know it. And wished she didn't.

She wanted to be a success in her chosen career, something she'd worked toward for years. But she also wanted her life to be intertwined with Tate's. Forever. She wanted them to make decisions together. Live together. Make babies. Have a long, happy life. Together.

But she knew that B.J. wasn't the only person who saw things differently—who saw that she and Tate would probably go their own ways soon, him back to his real life in Atlanta and her on to...wherever. No, B.J. wasn't the only one who saw that. She saw it, too, even if she didn't want to.

And Tate saw it.

She had been distressed a couple of days earlier when Tate had pointed out that he might be going home soon. She wasn't upset that he was going; she was upset because he hadn't said a word about taking her with him.

"Just because I'll be leaving doesn't mean that you have to do the same," Tate had said. "I wouldn't be selfish enough to ask you."

Ask me. Ask me! she had silently cried.

But he didn't.

She'd known all along that the adventure, the dream they'd shared, had to end sometime. But did it have to be so soon?

"You're in love with him, aren't you?" B.J. asked.

Maggie jumped, caught off guard by his abrupt question. "What?"

"Tell me to mind my own business. But you're in love with Tate."

"Mind your own business, B.J."

"Judging by the looks of things, I'd say he's in love with you, too."

She shook her head. "No."

"Tate's never been one to show his feelings. Keeps things bottled up. But that doesn't mean he doesn't care. If anything, he cares about things too much." B.J. hesitated. "I'd hate to see him hurt."

"So would I, B.J. So would I. And you were right about one thing. I do love him."

"Does he know?"

"No! And if you tell him, I'll call you a liar to your face."

"Why?"

"Because he has a whole other life back in North Georgia, and it doesn't include me." Tate himself had made that abundantly clear to her.

"But if you two truly love each other..."

"That hasn't been determined. Neither you nor I know for sure how Tate feels."

"Still—"

"And I have my own career to think of, too, as you pointed out a minute ago."

They both fell silent.

"Do you want me to put you in touch with the people I know in Nashville?" B.J. finally asked.

Maggie took a deep breath. B.J.'s offer could come to nothing. Or it could lead to her big break.

"I'm not sure," she said. Even as she said the words, she was calling herself all kinds of an idiot for not jumping at the chance he offered.

B.J. wrote a name and address on a piece of paper and handed it to her. "Here. Just in case. And be sure to use my name."

"I appreciate it, B.J.," she added, touching his hand. "But let me think about it. Okay?"

"Sure," he said, covering her hand with his. "And will you keep one thing in mind? I know it's not an easy decision for you—deciding between Tate and a career— even though you say he hasn't asked you to. And I believe you. It would be just like Tate not to tell you how he feels, especially if he cares a lot. He's a stubborn cuss. But he's one of the best, Maggie. He's certainly the finest man I've ever known.

"I guess what I'm trying to say is . . . Don't give up on him. Not if you love him." B.J. paused. "At least, try not to hurt him."

Maggie saw the unusual brightness in the eyes of the big, gruff, ex-football star. His concern touched her, more than she would have imagined. "Hurting Tate is the last thing on earth I want to do, B.J. I promise you, I'll try to do what's best for both of us."

He nodded, then averted his eyes as he quickly got up. "I just remembered some things I need to do in the kitchen," he said.

"B.J., there's a guy over here says he wants to talk to you."

Maggie hadn't heard or seen the bartender, Sam, approach their table. But there he was, standing right beside them, and she wondered how much of their conversation he'd heard. She hadn't trusted Sam the first time she saw him. And she hadn't changed her opinion since then.

"What guy?" B.J. asked.

"Standing at the end of the bar," Sam said, not turning around to look.

Maggie looked. The man at the bar was tall and swarthy, dressed in a business suit that was conspicuously out of place in the casual atmosphere of B.J.'s on the Beach.

"Did he say what he wanted?" B.J. asked.

Sam shrugged. "Not to me."

"I'll see you later, Maggie," B.J. said, heading for the bar.

She nodded and pretended to study her crossword puzzle. But all her senses had sprung to full alert the moment she saw the man at the bar. She had no way of knowing who he was or why he was here. Nevertheless, she would have bet everything she owned that his presence had something to do with Tate.

She just knew it. Felt it in her bones.

She strained to hear what the man and B.J. were discussing, but couldn't make out the words. Their voices were too low.

She propped her elbow on the table and covered her forehead with her open hand. Glancing through her fingers, she saw the two men in deep discussion. B.J. was smiling, but his body seemed tightly coiled—tense and wary.

Or was that her imagination, a reflection of the way she felt? Her mouth was dry and her palms were wet.

She saw the man pull a piece of paper from his breast pocket and hand it to B.J., who looked at it for some time. Then B.J. shook his head and said something while he returned the paper to the man.

She still couldn't hear his words, but thought she detected a new urgency in his voice. But that could have been her imagination, too.

After a few more minutes of talk, the man shook hands with B.J. and left the building. Maggie hoped that B.J. would come over and talk to her then...perhaps even tell her what had happened.

He didn't.

He never even glanced in her direction.

Instead, he walked around behind the bar and drew himself a glass of seltzer. He took a deep drink, then another one. After a moment, he walked to the other end of the bar, where he started talking to Sam.

Maggie took a deep breath and let it out. Maybe she'd been imagining things. Maybe there was nothing sinister about the strange man's visit to the bar, after all. It wouldn't be the first time she worried about things that had no basis in fact.

She shook her head and made a rueful grimace. Then she turned her attention back to the crossword.

"Maggie."

She looked up and saw B.J. standing beside her table.

"I brought you a soda," he said softly.

"I don't—"

"Pretend you want it," he said quietly. "Smile and say thank you."

She did what he said.

"Now," B.J. said, still in that strangely quiet voice, "I want you to keep on smiling. Nod occasionally...and for God's sake, try not to give anything away. Sam might be watching."

She nodded, smiling, trying to control the sudden fear that gripped her.

"That's good," B.J. said. "Just keep it up, and keep your eyes on me. Okay?"

She nodded again.

"That man who was just in here...you know the one."

She nodded again.

"He's with the FBI. He's looking for Tate."

Chapter Thirteen

Maggie gasped.

"Watch it!" B.J. said in a fierce whisper. "And smile."

"Sorry," she said, baring her teeth in what, from a distance, she could only hope would appear to be a smile.

"That's better," B.J. said. "Now listen. It's not as bad as you might think. They don't know for sure that Tate's in this area. They're simply checking all possibilities and came to see me because I'm an old friend."

"That's all?"

"Yeah. The guy showed me a picture and I told him I hadn't seen that man in years."

"Was it a picture of Tate?"

"Yes. But I told him the truth. The photo he showed me must have been ten years old, and sure as hell doesn't look like Tate does now."

Maggie nodded. "Did he believe you?"

"I'm almost certain he did. But that doesn't mean he might not come back here to check again. We need to warn Tate. Give me directions, and I'll drive out to where he works."

Maggie gave him directions, resisting the impulse to look at her watch. "It's late. He'll be getting off soon."

"I'll hurry. But if I miss him there, I'll catch him at the motel where you're staying. I'm sure he'll go there to clean up before he comes here."

Maggie shook her head. "I don't know where we're staying."

"What the hell are you talking about?"

"We take our belongings with us when we leave every day, and then Tate checks us into a different motel before he comes here to pick me up."

B.J. frowned. "How long has that been going on?"

"A long time. Since right after we got here."

"I'd better get going right away."

"Wait!" Maggie said. She quickly told him about the secret code she and Tate had devised.

"That was a good idea. It might come in handy," B.J. said.

Then he was gone. And there was nothing left for Maggie to do but worry.

She was fast becoming an expert at that.

MAGGIE WAS ALREADY halfway through her first show by the time B.J. returned. Catching her attention, he made a brief negative gesture with his head. But she'd known he had bad news anyway, simply by looking at his face.

He'd been gone so long, she figured he must have been driving up and down the beach trying to spot Tate's pickup truck at a motel after missing him at the construction site. She hadn't thought to tell him that Tate often parked the truck in a spot well away from the place where they were staying for the night. He said it decreased the chances of their being rudely awakened in the middle of the night.

Although she was as jittery as a cat in a thunderstorm, Maggie forced a smile as she kept on singing. She was trying to please the audience, and putting on a brave front as much for herself as for B.J. at the same time.

Her smile was genuine by the time she started the last number she'd do before intermission. She wanted desperately to talk to B.J. during the break between sets. They'd be able to reassure each other, and also to discuss plans to ensure Tate's safety.

All that changed in an instant. Everything changed when *he* walked into the crowded bar. The same FBI agent who'd thrown the world upside down this afternoon.

Maggie missed a beat, but quickly recovered. She scanned the room almost frantically, searching for B.J. When she finally spotted him, he was already making his way toward the FBI man.

She allowed herself a momentary sigh of relief, which was followed almost immediately by a new wave of panic. This was the last song before a scheduled forty-minute break for her and the backup band.

But she couldn't leave the room.

Not now.

Not when Tate might stroll into sight at any moment!

She was confident that B.J. could distract the government agent, but she needed to be here, too, to warn Tate of the danger. Her mind raced frantically as she tried to think . . . to consider all the possibilities.

She finished the song to enthusiastic applause. Without bothering to acknowledge it, she turned around to the band. "Guys, I need a big favor," she said. "A *huge* favor. Could we go directly into the next set without a break?"

They all started grumbling at once.

"I gotta have a cigarette."

"What? You want me to pee all over the floor?"

"C'mon, Maggie."

"Please," she pleaded. "I wouldn't ask you if it wasn't important." The musicians continued complaining. Then she had a sudden flash of inspiration.

"It's my grandmother," she said, catching their attention. "I didn't want to tell you, but she's at death's door and I want to finish early, so that I can see her just one last time before... before..."

The complaints immediately turned into sympathetic murmurs. Apologies.

"Dammit, Maggie. You should have told us before."

"And you shouldn't even have to ask. Of course, we'll stay."

"Let's hit it, guys."

So they started the second set without taking a break. Maggie caught a brief glimpse of surprise on B.J.'s face before he realized what was going on. Then he nodded his approval.

Maggie sang one song. Then another one. The minutes ticked by. She started to worry even more than before.

The FBI agent here wasn't the only one in town. They were probably all over the place. Maybe one of them had already caught up with Tate.

Or maybe this guy wasn't FBI, after all. Maybe he worked for the crooked financial consortium. And maybe his cohorts were questioning Tate at this very moment... grilling him underneath a harsh, overhead light, getting mean and nasty, slapping him around just to show him who was boss.

Tate stepped into the room.

Maggie stopped singing. Stopped breathing.

She had to warn him. Now.

"Granny's sick!" she yelled at the top of her lungs. Tate looked at her, not moving. "Granny's near death!" she added.

Tate disappeared, leaving the room as swiftly and silently as he'd entered it.

Maggie took a couple of quick, deep gulps of air. Her heart was thundering.

And the audience was looking at her. Staring. As if they all thought she'd gone completely bonkers.

She supposed she had gone a little crazy, in a sense, although she couldn't explain that to the audience. Still, she had to tell them something.

"I apologize," she finally said. "I, uh, learned the bad news today and . . . uh, I suddenly couldn't hold it in any longer. I'm sorry."

Was that enough of an explanation? she wondered. Too much? Nobody in the audience had moved. They were all still watching her. Probably waiting to see what crazy thing she'd do next.

"You see, my grandmother has always been special to me. She was the one person I could always count on to be there for me when I needed her, giving me a hug and a comforting word."

Enough is enough, she decided, getting off the stool where she'd been sitting. If she piled on any more syrup, she'd probably make everyone in the room sick, herself included.

"So, if you don't mind, I'd like to dedicate this next song to my granny."

She took a deep breath, motioned behind her back for the band not to play along, and started singing "Amazing Grace." She was a little nervous at first, wondering how the audience would react. Then she reminded herself that she wasn't doing this for the audience. She was doing it for Tate. That thought helped, and she gathered strength and courage as she went along.

When she finished, she lowered her head, touching her chin to her chest. Waiting. Nobody said a word. Or moved. Or made a sound. The room was so silent, she wondered if anybody was even breathing.

She must have been really bad, so bad that the audience didn't know what to do, she thought with a sinking feeling. But at least she'd accomplished what she'd set out to do, which was to help Tate escape.

Still . . . she couldn't help but wish . . .

All at once, as if on cue, the audience burst into thunderous applause. Maggie lifted her head. They were getting up from their chairs, standing. Everybody in the room. Cheering wildly. Some of them even crying.

She couldn't believe it.

She'd never seen anything like it.

As soon as the show was over, Maggie stopped by her dressing room only long enough to hurriedly remove her costume and change into shorts and a shirt. Then she sneaked out the back door to go in search of Tate.

Please let him be at our meeting place waiting for me.

She probably should have told B.J. where she was going, but she didn't want to waste time tracking him down. And for all she knew, the FBI man might still be around.

Besides, she and Tate could phone B.J. later to let him know they were safe. And together.

Please let it be so.

She ran almost all the way, only slowing down when she approached their prearranged meeting place. She forced herself to take the time to do a few cool-down stretching exercises, so anyone watching would think she'd been jogging on the beach.

Then she headed for the beachfront cabana, casually kicking up sand as she walked. In her mind, she repeated the same word over and over. *Please. Please.*

The night was warm and balmy, with barely a breeze and only a sliver of a moon. The cabana was shadowed, silent, and she saw no sign of Tate. The only sound she heard was the hammering of her own heart. She walked to the far end of the beach house and rounded a corner.

Suddenly, from the shadows, a man reached out to grab her from behind. His muscular arm pulled her against his chest and his callused hand covered her mouth. She was filled with a terror she'd never known before, had only read about.

"Sorry," he said. "It's only me."

Tate.

Maggie closed her eyes, sagging against his chest. She probably would have fallen if he hadn't been holding her so tightly. He removed his hand from her mouth, turned her around in his arms and started kissing her...her lips, her nose, her eyelids, her cheeks, her neck.

She wound her arms around his neck, holding on for dear life, and returned his kisses. Kiss for kiss.

Neither of them spoke.

Words weren't necessary. Not now. Not yet.

They could talk later.

SHE TOLD HIM about the FBI agent, and about B.J.'s frantic search to find Tate. She told him how the government man had returned to the bar...and how she'd tried to explain her wild outburst to the audience after Tate had heard her warning and left. "They thought I was looney-tunes, for sure. And I was for a minute or two there."

Tate kissed her some more. Then they went to a pay phone and Tate called B.J. to tell him they were okay. After that, they drove to the motel where he had rented rooms for the night.

Maggie hesitated at her door. "Tate...please don't make me stay alone tonight."

"I won't," he said after warring with himself for only a brief moment. "Just give me a couple of minutes to park the truck down the street. Then to hell with everybody else. I'm not letting you out of my sight."

He was surprised to find Maggie already in bed when he returned to her room. "Are you tired?" he asked.

"No. And I'm not sleepy, either, in case that was your next question."

He lifted his eyebrows. Then, as her meaning dawned, he nodded. He tugged his shirt loose from his trousers and started unbuttoning it. Slowly. Deliberately. One button at a time. When he was finished, he took off the shirt and threw it in the general direction of the chair.

He watched Maggie the entire time.

And she watched him.

He kicked off his shoes. He wasn't wearing socks. He unbuttoned the top of his Levi's, then slowly lowered the zipper. Lifting first one leg, then the other, he pulled off the jeans and his briefs at the same time, leaving them on the floor.

Maggie's blue eyes were dark, glittering in the semi-darkness.

Slowly, still not speaking, he moved to the bed. He leaned over her and pulled back the light covers. She was totally, breathtakingly beautiful in her nakedness. He lay down beside her, not touching. He was almost afraid to touch her.

He was totally aroused. Painfully so. He wanted to bury himself inside her, up to the hilt. Again and again. But he knew she might not feel the same way.

After a moment, he reached across the distance separating them, gently pushing back a tendril of dark hair from her forehead with one finger. He swallowed.

"Are you ready for me, Maggie?" he whispered.

"More than."

And she was.

She shifted her body closer, offering him everything she had—sweetness and passion, strength and life. It was everything he'd ever wanted.

They made love with an intensity Tate had never known before, never imagined even in his dreams. It was almost as if both of them knew this might be the last time they'd come together like this.

In this lifetime.

And when it was over, when they'd collapsed side by side on the bed in limp, damp exhaustion, Tate felt a deep sorrow he'd never known before, either. Because sometime soon—either tomorrow or the next day after or next week—Maggie would be gone.

He might never see her again.

"YOU DIDN'T TELL ME that the audience tonight was in tears after you sang 'Amazing Grace,'" Tate said.

Maggie lifted her head from his chest. "What?"

"B.J. told me about it over the phone. He said he'd never seen anything like it. Why didn't you tell me?"

She shrugged. "What could I say? Anything I said would sound like bragging."

"Bragging's allowed. Especially when it's deserved."

"I'll admit I was flattered. But it's really not that big of a deal . . . not in the whole scheme of things."

"Maggie," he chided, shaking his head, then giving her a hug. She sighed, settling against his chest again.

"You also didn't tell me that B.J. offered to introduce you to some important contacts he has in Nashville."

She sat up in bed. "He blabs a lot, doesn't he?"

"No. But he is my best friend. He thought I'd like to know about it."

"And do you?" she asked, almost angrily. "Want to know, that is?"

"Of course I want to know. This is important, Maggie."

"Really? Why is it so important to you, Tate?"

Was she deliberately trying to hurt him?

"Because I care about you, dammit!" he said, growing angry himself.

"That's the first I've heard of it."

"You had to know."

"Not if you didn't tell me. And you've never said a word."

"I'm saying it now! I care for you! More than..." He stopped abruptly and took a couple of deep breaths. He had to be careful here and try not to push her too far. He didn't want to say something that would force her to make a commitment she'd regret later.

"More than you think," he finished lamely.

He loved Maggie with all his heart. He wanted her to go back to Georgia with him, wanted them to be married and live together always. If she loved him the same way, she'd do it. But it had to be something she really wanted, too. Otherwise, she'd come to hate him sometime down the road for talking her into giving up her dream.

And he'd hate himself even more for doing that to her.

"I want you to be happy, Maggie," he said, touching her cheek with the backs of his fingers. "That's all."

"Thank you," she whispered, briefly brushing her lips against his hand. "And Tate, I think you already know it but just to make it official . . . I care for you, too."

He nodded, and after a moment cleared his throat. "So. Are you going to take B.J. up on his offer?"

"I don't know," she replied slowly. She didn't look at him. "Maybe." A heartbeat later, she added, "Probably."

Tate's throat ached. His eyes burned.

He nodded again.

MAGGIE WAS still asleep when Tate silently slipped out of the motel early the next morning. He carried his suit—the same one he'd worn the first night he met her—under his arm in a brown paper bag. Pushing his dark glasses up higher on his nose, he walked quickly to the motel down the street where he'd left the truck.

After dropping the suit off at a one-hour cleaners, he visited a drugstore, where he made several purchases. Then he drove around until he spotted a barber shop, where he had both his hair and his beard neatly trimmed. Next he visited a department store and bought himself a new dress shirt, socks and tie. By then, it was time to pick up his suit.

On his way back to the motel, he stopped off long enough to buy some freshly squeezed orange juice, hot doughnuts and coffee. Maggie was still in bed when he let himself back into her motel room.

"Tate?" she said sleepily. "Are you on your way out?"

"Nope," he replied. "Just coming back in. I brought hot coffee and doughnuts. Want some?"

"Mmm. I could be talked into that." She got out of bed and headed for the bathroom.

Tate smiled at the sight of her naked back—beautiful and flawless. Female perfection. He admired the totally natural, unselfconscious way she handled nudity, too, hers or his.

The fact was, he liked almost everything about Maggie Bennett.

He'd hung his suit in the closet and spread out his purchases on the dresser by the time Maggie returned. She was wearing her thigh-length T-shirt, but her long legs were still uncovered.

"My, but you've been busy," she said, gesturing to Tate's purchases. "And you've had your hair cut, too!" she exclaimed. "And your beard!"

"Yes to all three," he said, fingering his beard. "What do you think?"

"Very handsome," she replied, nodding her approval. "What's the occasion?"

"I'm going calling," he said, handing her a cup of coffee, black with no sugar, the way she liked it. "I plan to visit Mr. Lloyd Garvey at the chicken processing plant today."

Her eyes widened. "You thought of a plan to get inside?"

"Not merely *a* plan. It's a wonderful, marvelous, stupendous plan!"

"I can hardly wait. Tell me about it."

"I'm going to put on my freshly cleaned suit, my new shirt and tie..." He picked up a pair of tortoiseshell glasses from the dresser. "And these new eyeglasses—with clear lenses, of course. Then, after I've prevailed upon you to dye my hair and beard again—for the last time, I hope—I'm going to present myself at the processing plant as a government inspector!"

Maggie's mouth dropped open.

"It occurred to me in the middle of the night last night when I was thinking about that FBI agent. All of a sudden I remembered all the government men I know. You wouldn't believe the number of inspectors who visit a chicken processing plant."

She frowned. "It sounds like it might work... But can you really pull it off? I mean, can you get away with the deception?"

"After all the government inspectors I've dealt with in my lifetime? It should be a piece of cake." He laughed. "And speaking of cake... have a doughnut."

After breakfast, Maggie looked at the new coloring Tate had bought for his hair. "This is darker than what we used before," she said, reading the instructions on the package.

"I couldn't remember the exact shade. Will this do?"

"It's pretty dark."

"I hate to waste the time it'll take to exchange it. Let's try it anyway. We can always get something else if it doesn't work out."

She shrugged. "It's your hair."

"Well?" Tate asked when Maggie had finally finished the job.

She tilted her head while she studied him. "It's really dark... makes you look different."

"Isn't that what we wanted?"

"I mean *really* different. Your own mother wouldn't know—" She stopped in midsentence. "Sorry. Bad choice of words."

"It's okay," he said. "Really. I don't hate her or anything."

"I still think . . ."

"I know. And I'll admit I was pretty hurt at first. But like you told me before, maybe she had a good reason for what she did."

"I hope so, Tate."

"So do I, Maggie." He took a deep breath. "And now it's time for me to get ready for my big appointment."

After he'd finished dressing, he stood for Maggie's inspection. She straightened his tie and then smiled. "You look wonderful."

"I'll bet you say that to all the guys." His voice was husky.

"Sure do," she said in a tone that echoed his.

"Listen. I'll probably be back here before it's time to check out. But in case I'm not—"

"Don't take the risk of coming to B.J.'s bar!"

"I won't. I'll hide out for the rest of the day, and then meet you at our secret place on the beach. Okay?"

She nodded. "Please be careful."

"You, too." He kissed her quickly and then rushed out of the room, terrified that he'd make a fool of himself if he didn't get away fast.

"EVERYTHING SEEMS to be in good shape, Mr. Garvey," Tate said.

"Lloyd. I already told you to call me Lloyd."

"Sorry, I forgot. Lloyd. As I told you, I don't find any health code violations. You operate a clean, tight, sanitary plant."

Tate deliberately paused for effect. "Frankly, I don't see how you manage to do it, considering the condition of your equipment. In fact, I don't see how you manage to keep some of that equipment running at all. By all rights, it should have been retired years ago."

To Tate's surprise, Lloyd Garvey laughed. "That's the truth! By all rights, the machinery *and* I should have been retired by now. But I got me a couple of top-notch mechanics to keep the machinery running."

"And how about you, Lloyd? What keeps you running?"

Garvey shook his head. "Necessity."

"I don't understand."

"My daddy built this plant. When he died, he left it to me. He left another plant just like it to my twin brother, Floyd, up in Birmingham."

So, Tate thought. *The plot thickens.*

"We both tried to carry on in Daddy's footsteps, doing things the same way he'd have done—minding our business, not doing harm to another poor soul, treating everybody else the way we'd expect them to treat us."

"The Golden Rule," Tate said.

"Yes. That's the way Daddy ran the business, and it's the way Floyd and I always ran the business." Garvey ran his fingers through his thinning white hair. "Then, when it was about time for Floyd and me to retire a couple of years ago, we found us a nice little bit of acreage down on the beach near Destin.

"We decided to buy it together and build side by side. Sort of a compound like the Kennedys have, but on a smaller scale," Garvey said with a laugh. "A place where our kids and grandkids could all congregate in our retirement years."

"It sounds wonderful," Tate said.

"That's what Floyd and I both thought. We talked with the real estate agent and he put us in touch with the owner of the property—an outfit called Midsouth Investment Company."

Oh no! Tate thought.

"We talked to Midsouth and explained our situation to them—told 'em how we were both looking to sell our plants before we retired—and they said, 'Whoa. Don't make any hasty decisions here. We might be able to work out a deal that'd be good for all of us.' What it boiled down to is that Floyd and I would get the retirement property and a tidy little bit of cash, and Midsouth would hold an option on both our processing plants. Anything they made off the sale of the plants above the value of our property would be theirs to keep. It sounded like a good deal to Floyd and me, so we signed a whole bunch of papers."

Garvey took a deep breath. "The first hitch came when we applied for a permit to build on our wonderful beachfront property. It turned out that Midsouth didn't own it, after all. They only had an option on it...same as they had on our processing plants."

"They lied to you," Tate whispered.

"They sure as hell did. But by the time we found out, they'd tied up my plant and Floyd's in court, tight as a drum. We couldn't sell to anybody else, couldn't do anything with our own damn property. At least, not until after Midsouth's option expired."

Tate caught his breath. "And, uh, when will that be?"

Suddenly, unexpectedly, Lloyd Garvey grinned. "Three months ago," he said with a deep chuckle. "Know anybody who wants to buy a chicken processing plant?"

Tate didn't laugh along with him. "I might."

Mr. Garvey's grin disappeared. "What's that you say?"

"Mr. Garvey...Lloyd," Tate said, taking a deep breath, "I'm going to tell you a remarkable story about how Midsouth falsely claimed to own your plant in order to effect a merger with another company. I know it'll sound farfetched at first, but I hope you'll hear me out. I'm taking a big gamble by telling you at all.''

Lloyd Garvey didn't speak, didn't move a muscle, didn't show any kind of reaction at all. Tate's heart was in his throat as he forced himself to continue. "To begin with, I gave you a false name earlier. My name is really Tate Rabun . . .''

YES. Tate thought. *Yes.*

"Yes!" he shouted, waving his fist outside the window of the pickup truck. "By damn, I did it!"

He honked his horn at an oncoming car, leaned out the window. "I did it!" he yelled at the startled driver. The man immediately sent him a bird in return. Tate laughed.

He might have felt better in his life, but if he had, he couldn't remember when it was. *"Yes!"* he said again, wishing Maggie were here to share his joy.

He speeded up, eager to get home to tell her about it. He'd never have been able to do it without her. Maggie. The love of his life.

Maybe, now that things were looking up for him, looking great in fact, he might get up the nerve to tell her exactly how he felt about her.

But no. His success didn't change the fact that she was still searching for her own. And he still wouldn't be the one to try to talk her out of what she'd wanted and worked for for so long.

Even so, he could give her a small token of his appreciation, couldn't he? Flowers? Yes! He owed her that, at least, even though he wanted to ask and give much more.

Flowers it is, he thought, starting to look for a shop.

Some miles later, he found one and went inside, ordering a lavish bouquet. He was grinning when he came back outside and headed for the truck. On the way, he passed several newspaper vending machines. He stopped at one, reached into his pocket for a coin, dropped it into the slot and pulled out a paper.

He opened the door, climbed into the truck, put the newspaper on the seat beside him and then carefully placed the bouquet on top of the paper. He glanced down at the bouquet, smiling. Then something caught his eye. He reached over and pulled the newspaper out from beneath the flowers.

Maggie smiled at him from the front page.

He blinked and read the caption under her picture, which wasn't ten years old like the one of him that the FBI had shown B.J., but a recent publicity shot furnished by the Green Lantern, the tavern where she'd been singing at the time he disappeared.

"Nightclub singer," Tate read aloud, "possibly involved in kidnapping of prominent businessman." He clenched the paper, blinking rapidly as it started to blur and he could only make out disjointed words and phrases. *Maggie Bennett . . . prime suspect, wanted for questioning . . . five-state alert.*

He closed his eyes.

"Oh, Maggie. What have I done to you?"

Chapter Fourteen

By noon, Maggie was feeling claustrophobic in the dinky little motel room. She decided to go to the beach for a few hours, then on to B.J.'s bar, where she could wait until it was time for her show. Anything was better than hibernating here.

She put on her bathing suit and a short terry robe. Tate had kept most of their personal belongings with him in the truck. Maggie stuffed what was left into a tote bag and left the key on the dresser.

She felt better as soon as she was outside. The day was perfect—bright sunshine with only a few fleecy high clouds, and a nice onshore breeze. She rented a beach chair with umbrella, went for a short swim, then applied suntan lotion and settled down for a comfy little nap.

TATE BROUGHT the pickup to a screeching stop in front of the motel. He was out of the car and running before the engine died.

Rounding a corner, he had a sinking feeling as soon as he saw the cleaning cart parked outside the door to the room he and Maggie had shared last night. He raced ahead anyway. A maid was inside the room, making the bed.

"The woman," he said breathlessly. "The woman who stayed here last night. Have you seen her?"

The maid shook her head. "Nobody here but me."

Tate glanced at the door to the bathroom.

"Nobody there, either," the maid said. "I already cleaned it."

"Thank you." Tate turned around and started walking rapidly toward the pay phone just outside the motel office. Depositing his quarter, he dialed a number, and was relieved when he heard a familiar voice answer.

"B.J.," Tate said. "I'm glad I got you. I—"

"Yeah, Tom. It's nice to hear from you, too," B.J. said.

Tate hesitated. "I guess you heard about . . . our mutual acquaintance."

"Yeah. So did a lot of other people."

B.J. must be talking about cops, Tate decided. "You've had a lot of visitors?"

"That's for sure."

"They still there?"

"Yep."

"How about our friend? Have you seen . . . ?"

"Not today."

Tate felt a quick surge of adrenaline. If Maggie wasn't at the bar and wasn't here, maybe she'd learned about the danger she was in and had gone into hiding. Maybe. "I'll see what I can find out," he told B.J.

"Can I call you back?" B.J. asked.

"Not here. I'll call you later and tell you where."

Tate drove to the condo where his and Maggie's meeting place was located. Leaving the pickup in the parking lot, he walked around the condo, past the pool and on to the cabana. There was no sign of Maggie, but then he really hadn't expected her to be there so soon.

Walking back to the truck, he suddenly realized he was attracting a lot of attention because he was still dressed in his suit and tie. He decided to take time to change clothes. He drove to a nearby service station, where he changed into shorts, a shirt and sneakers. Then he started searching for Maggie in earnest.

MAGGIE WOKE UP from her nap hot and thirsty. The sun had sunk lower in the sky while she was asleep and now was beaming almost directly on her. She readjusted the umbrella and that helped a little, but she was still thirsty.

There was a motel directly behind the spot where she was sitting on the beach. Maybe she could find something there to drink. She left her tote bag in the beach chair and walked up to the motel, where she found an outdoor fountain beside the pool and drank her fill.

The pool looked inviting, too. A sign said it was for registered guests only, but how would anyone know whether or not she was registered? She went for a long swim, then played at the shallow end for a while with two little girls and their mother. Finally, she went back to her beach chair, readjusted the umbrella again and pulled out a book to read.

"B.J.?" TATE SAID. "This is Tom again. Any news?"

"No. Sorry." His voice sounded even more guarded than it had been the first time Tate called.

"Me, too. But I'm ready to give you that phone number now."

"Okay," B.J. said.

Tate gave him the number of the pay phone where he was.

"One more time," B.J. said after he'd finished.

"You're not writing it down?"

"No."

"Good," Tate said. He repeated the number.

"Give me a few minutes," B.J. said. Then he hung up.

Tate looked at the receiver he still held in his hand. After a moment, he hung up, too. Then he started pacing while he waited for B.J. to call him back.

After an eternity—which surprisingly registered less than ten minutes on Tate's watch—the phone rang. He grabbed it in midring. "Hello."

"That was fast," B.J. said. "You have any luck finding Maggie?"

"No. I must have been up and down this part of the beach a dozen times. There's no sign of her. Maybe the cops have already picked her up."

"I don't think so. My place is still crawling with them, the same way it's been since early this morning. If they'd found her, they would have eased up by now."

"That's true. She probably read in the paper that she was wanted, and she went into hiding. If that's the case, I'm sure she'll be at our secret meeting place tonight," Tate said, with much more confidence than he felt.

"Yeah."

His friend's voice seemed to echo Tate's own misgivings. "What kind of cops are in on this?" he asked, changing the subject.

"Police, sheriff's department, FBI, state patrol... you name it. I was afraid they might have tapped my phone. That's why I was extra-cautious."

Tate whistled.

"There's worse," B.J. said. "They've set up roadblocks at both ends of the beach, so nobody gets in or out without them knowing it."

"Damn. If I do find Maggie...I mean, when I find her, I suppose the best thing to do would be to turn ourselves in immediately."

Tate waited. B.J. said nothing. "B.J.?" he finally asked.

"I'll be honest with you, Tate. Some of these cops I've seen today are young, inexperienced ... and way too eager."

The dread fear that had been following Tate all day finally caught up with him. "You mean you think it might be dangerous for us to turn ourselves in?"

"Yes," B.J. replied after a pause. "I do think it would be dangerous...especially for Maggie. Kidnapping is a serious charge."

"Don't you think I know that! Don't you think I've been calling myself all kinds of a stupid idiot and—"

"Tate! Calm down."

Tate took several deep breaths. "Sorry."

"You're forgiven. And it's understandable," B.J. said. "And besides that...I think I have a plan to get you two away from Panama City Beach. That way, you'll be able to turn yourselves in to more...uh...sympathetic law enforcement officers someplace else."

"I'm listening," Tate said.

"A friend of mine has a boat—sleek, high-powered and fast as hell. And he owes me a favor."

Tate continued listening as B.J. outlined a plan for a midnight rendezvous, and felt a glimmer of hope. But it still wasn't enough to ease the tension in his gut that had been steadily building for hours.

MAGGIE YAWNED and stretched. She smiled, feeling contented with herself and the world at large. What a marvelously relaxing day it had been! She stretched again, looking out over the gentle swells of the Gulf of Mexico as the bright orange sun disappeared on the horizon.

She sighed, knowing it was time for her to disappear, too. She needed to get up and make her way down the beach to B.J.'s bar, where she'd barely have time to grab a bite to eat, shower and change into her costume for the first show.

Reluctantly, she sat up in her beach chair. She took one last lingering look at the multicolored hues of the horizon. A man walked past, blocking her view for a moment. He was a tall man. Dark. Vaguely familiar.

"Tate?"

She hadn't realized she'd said the word out loud until the man stopped dead in his tracks. He wheeled around. It *was* Tate.

"Tate. What on earth . . . ?"

He was standing beside her before she could finish the sentence. "What are you doing here?" he said from between clenched teeth.

"Nothing." Why was he so angry? What did he expect her to be doing?

"Don't you know this place is crawling with cops?"

"Oh, dear," she said. "Are they looking for you?"

"No! They're looking for *you!*"

"Me? Why?"

"You're wanted for kidnapping! It's in all the papers."

"That's ridiculous. Who would I kidnap?"

"Me!"

TATE FINALLY managed to get Maggie away from full view of anybody who might happen by on the beach and into relative safety underneath a pier. He tried to explain the seriousness of their predicament, but she kept interrupting him with questions about what had happened at the processing plant that morning, so he told her.

"That's terrific!" she exclaimed. "You have those crooks dead to rights."

"Yeah. I was planning to go up to Birmingham and talk to Mr. Garvey's brother, Floyd, in order to drive that last nail into their coffin, but I decided to put that idea on hold."

"What on earth for?"

Again, he tried to explain their predicament. And again, Maggie kept interrupting. "The cops have been after you for ages," she pointed out. "And now they're after me, too. What's the difference?"

"It's my family and board of directors who are looking for me, Maggie," he explained . . . fairly patiently, he thought, considering the circumstances. "It's the cops in five states that are after you! Kidnapping is a serious crime!"

"But we both know I didn't do it."

"We know it, but the police don't. We have to find a way to keep you safe until we can surrender and tell them the whole story." Then he outlined B.J.'s plan for their escape by boat.

"That sounds like fun." she said.

"What's happened to you?" he said, frowning. "You're the one who always worries so much. About everything."

She shrugged. "I guess I finally worried myself out. I had a great time on the beach today."

"You were out in the open. In broad daylight. Hundreds of different people could have recognized you. The police could have arrested you or..." He didn't finish the rest of his sentence.

"But none of that happened, did it?"

"Not today," he admitted. "But we still have several hours to go before it's time for the boat to pick us up. We'll need to find someplace better than this to hide out."

Maggie nodded, and furrowed her brow while she thought. Suddenly she grinned. "The amusement park across the street."

Tate glanced at her in astonishment. "You're out of your mind."

"No. We talked about it before, remember? You can either hide out in a remote place—and this beach has precious few of those—or you can lose yourself in a crowd. I was out here in a crowd of people all day, and nothing happened. Nobody recognized me. And if any cops came by, I didn't see them. They probably didn't bother coming out here because nobody would expect a fugitive to go where all the people are."

Thinking about it, Tate found himself agreeing with her. Maybe it was because he'd worried himself out, too. "Okay," he said, holding out his hand to her. "We'll try it."

They shook on it.

Then they strolled across the street, casual as could be, and lost themselves in the huge crowds at the Miracle Strip Amusement Park.

They rode the roller coaster and the Ferris wheel. She almost knocked him out of the park in the bumper cars, then hung on to him for dear life while they laughed and squealed their way through the haunted house.

They ate hot dogs and soft ice cream and cotton candy, after which Maggie almost got sick on the high swings. Then they rode the Ferris wheel again. And again. And again.

And they never saw a cop, except for the amusement park's security guard.

"Well, what do you think?" Maggie asked. They were at the very top of the Ferris wheel, in the highest seat. The wheel wasn't turning at the moment because new passengers were getting on board. But that was happening a world away from them . . . half a turn of the wheel away from them.

Tate looked down at the carnival crowd beneath them, then out to the glittering neon signs lining the Miracle Strip in both directions as far as the eye could see, and finally to one side where the dark expanse of the Gulf of Mexico ran still and deep. He felt the gentle sway of their seat high on top of the Ferris wheel, and the faint touch of an ocean breeze caressing his cheek, and breathed in the sweet smell of the woman beside him. "I think," he said, "that this is the most perfect moment of my life."

Later, when it was time for them to leave, they made their way back across the street with the same nonchalance they'd shown before. "Just two friends out for a late night stroll on the beach," Tate commented.

"What do we do about the truck with all our things in it?" Maggie asked.

"We leave it. Everything. Including the bouquet of flowers on the front seat. *That* should give the police something to think about," he added with a grin.

"Flowers?"

"I bought them for you earlier. To celebrate our success. That was before I saw your picture on the front page of the paper, of course."

"It was a nice thought, Tate. Thank you."

"You're welcome."

"So all we can carry is what we have on?"

"You should be thankful you're wearing a bathing suit to swim out to the boat."

"I suppose. But what about later, when we're on our way to Birmingham? This bikini could be a little chilly to travel in."

"I don't remember us agreeing that we'd even go to Birmingham."

"Of course, we'll go. You need to talk to Floyd Garvey, and I have no intention of missing out on the fun after all the time and effort I've invested in this thing. I'm planning on going back to Atlanta with you, too, by the way."

Tate considered the possibilities. He *did* want to talk to Floyd Garvey, and he'd feel a lot easier about Maggie if he knew she was with him. Not only that, but Lloyd Garvey had suggested a possibility he hadn't told Maggie about yet. He'd wanted to surprise her. "Okay," he said.

She narrowed her eyes. "You're agreeing with me? Just like that? What is it that you're not telling me?"

"Shut up before I change my mind," he said, taking her hand to pull her along the beach toward the fishing pier for their midnight rendezvous with B.J.'s friend and the fast boat.

Unfortunately the pier was too high to walk to the end and meet the boat. They would have to swim. In the shadows beneath it, Maggie removed her beach robe and sandals, and Tate took off his shirt and sneakers. The breeze, still blowing in from the Gulf, had stiffened, making them shiver. "I'll bet the water's cold," Maggie said.

"It's the same temperature it was earlier today. We'll be warmer as soon as we get in."

"What about after we get out?"

She had a point there. Then Tate spied a cord—probably a broken ski rope—that had wound itself around one of the pilings. "Tell you what," he said. "Let's put our shoes and your robe and my shirt inside your tote bag. I'll tie it to my back. Okay?"

After he secured the tote bag high up on his shoulders, which was actually against the back of his neck, Tate and Maggie waded out into the water, hand in hand, keeping to the shadows underneath the pier. "The water *is* warm," she whispered.

"I told you so."

"What about sharks?" she asked a moment later.

"We have enough things to worry about, Maggie. Don't look for more."

"The water's almost up to my neck," she said a little later.

"Okay," he said. "We'll start swimming. Remember to keep close to the pilings and grab onto one to rest if you get tired."

They swam. And swam. And swam. Tourist brochures claimed that the pier was a mile long. Now Tate believed the literature. "I'm tired," Maggie said finally.

"We'll rest for a moment," he readily agreed, reaching out for the piling closest to him. "Ouch!" he exclaimed, quickly pulling back his hand.

"What is it?"

"Barnacles. Sharp as broken glass. Don't touch the pilings, Maggie. Can you rest by treading water?"

"I think so. Did you hurt yourself?"

"Nah. Luckily, the hard labor I've been doing these past few weeks has built up a whole slew of calluses." They treaded water for a while. "Feeling better now?" he asked.

"Great," she replied. "Let's go."

They started swimming again but Tate watched Maggie closely and after a short while he knew she'd been lying when she claimed she was rested and ready to go. She was nearing exhaustion. "Hold up," he said. "Let's rest again."

"Is something wrong?"

"I want to readjust your tote bag," he lied. "Here," he added, taking her wrists and placing her hands on his shoulder. "Hold on to me while I rearrange things."

He made unnecessary adjustments to the tote bag while Maggie rested. "I think that does it," he said after a while.

She looked at him. "Tate."

"What?"

"Thanks."

"For what?"

She shook her head and started swimming again. He followed her.

They finally reached the end of the pier but there was no boat in sight. By Tate's calculations, B.J.'s friend should have been here by now.

"What next?" Maggie asked.

"We wait for the boat," Tate said. "It's a little early for him to be here yet."

So they waited, treading water as they did so. And they waited, while Tate grew more anxious by the moment. Damn it all! Where was the boat? And how much longer could they stay out here? And suppose the boat didn't come at all?

"Tate?"

He heard the concern in Maggie's voice. "It's okay. There's nothing to worry about. The boat should be here soon."

Soon? It should already be here! Ages ago.

"I think I hear it now," she said a moment later.

Tate listened, but didn't hear a thing except the sound of waves lapping against the pilings. "Me, too," he lied, hoping to keep Maggie's spirits up. And then he *did* hear it. A boat. Going full-out. Coming closer.

The speedboat pulled to an abrupt stop directly in front of the pier, then made a small circle a bit to the right. Tate saw the signal from a flashlight—two long, one short, two long.

"Let's go!" he said. They started swimming.

It was hard to tell which of them was more surprised when it was Sam the bartender who pulled them aboard the sleek boat. "I don't like you any more than I did in the beginning," Sam said succinctly. "But I owe B.J. my life."

THE LATE-MODEL Chevy was parked exactly where B.J. had told Tate it would be, and the keys were in the place he'd said they would be. Maggie got in the passenger side, Tate in the driver's side, and he threw the tote bag on the seat between them.

He didn't even take the time to put on his shirt until they were well outside of town, on the road north to Montgomery and, beyond that, Birmingham. They drove all night.

Tate relinquished the wheel to Maggie at about four in the morning, when his eyes wouldn't stay open any longer. He fell into a deep sleep as soon as she took over, but was wide-awake a little more than an hour later, and hungry as a bear. They stopped at an all-night diner to eat.

"You look cute in your little terry cloth beach robe," he said, pushing back his plate after he'd polished off steak and eggs, sliced tomatoes and hash brown potatoes, along with two orders of Texas toast and several cups of black coffee.

"I'll bet you say that to all the women when you're full of food and feeling good about yourself."

"I sure do," he agreed, lifting his coffee mug to her in a toast. "Are you ready to roll on to Birmingham now?"

She lifted her own mug. "You bet."

They made good time, arriving at the outskirts of the city just as the workday was beginning. "I'd better stop and call Mr. Garvey," Tate said. "Lloyd said his brother was expecting us, but I should make sure. I also need to get directions to his processing plant. Do you have a pencil?"

Maggie reached into her tote bag and pulled out both a pencil and a pad. "What else do you have in there?" Tate asked.

"Lots of things," she replied cryptically. "Including both our toothbrushes."

Tate lifted his eyebrows. "I knew I was wise to bring your tote bag along."

"Very." Maggie brushed her teeth and hair while Tate made his phone call. They met back at the Chevy.

"It's all set," he said. "Floyd's plant is on the other side of town in North Birmingham, but he said the media here hasn't mentioned my so-called kidnapping, so the police shouldn't be a problem."

"What about clothes?" she asked, gesturing to her skimpy beach robe that only came to midthigh.

"I told Floyd about the way we were dressed, but he said to come on anyway. He's anxious to get started. So am I," he added significantly.

Maggie shrugged. "I wouldn't want to interfere with big business."

Driving through rush-hour traffic, their progress was slow, frustratingly so. "Damn-fool drivers," Tate muttered when they finally parked at the processing plant in midmorning.

Maggie opened her eyes and released the death grip she held on the armrest. "I'm just glad we made it at all."

Floyd Garvey was waiting for them and immediately escorted them to his office. Even though they were twins, the Garvey brothers didn't resemble each other much at all, Tate decided. Probably it was because Floyd was completely bald, whereas his brother Lloyd had a full head of snow-white hair. Aside from looks, the Garvey boys were very much alike—open, honest and down-to-earth. Tate found himself responding to Floyd almost immediately, the same way he'd done with Lloyd.

Floyd made sure that Maggie was settled comfortably on the sofa in his office with refreshments and magazines before he got down to business with Tate. After leafing through the magazines for some time, Maggie quietly stretched out on the sofa and went to sleep. Tate glanced at her with a mixture of amusement and tenderness. He was happy she'd finally conked out. Unlike him, she'd been awake the entire night.

Tate woke her up for lunch, which Floyd ordered brought in from a nearby barbecue restaurant. Maggie ate sparingly, then excused herself and went back to the sofa. To sleep.

"Pretty young woman," Floyd commented.

"She's tired," Tate felt compelled to explain. "We drove all night." Then he and Floyd got back to business, hammering out the last details of their arrangement. By the time Maggie awoke again late in the afternoon, they had long since settled everything and were trading chicken stories.

"Well, look who's awake!" Floyd said. "And just in time for supper, too."

"Sorry I dozed off..." Maggie said, rubbing her eyes as she got up. Then, doing a double take, she asked. "What did you say? It's suppertime already?"

"Sure is," Floyd responded cheerfully. "I'll order us up a nice juicy steak with all the trimmings. How does that sound?"

Maggie looked at Tate. "Wonderful," she said. Tate nodded and gave her his biggest grin.

"And after we've finished eating," Floyd announced, "I'll call the sheriff."

Maggie's mouth dropped open in dismay.

"It's okay," Tate explained quickly. "The sheriff is a good friend of Floyd's. He's going to personally escort us back to Atlanta."

Tate gave Maggie a wink. "It's time for me to go back and face my own music now," he added. "Are you with me?"

"All the way," she replied with a grin.

Chapter Fifteen

Maggie fidgeted in her chair while she waited for Tate's mother and brother to arrive and the meeting to start. Tate had already introduced her to the other members of the SCFC board of directors. Her mouth twitched as she recalled the particular words he'd used: "My good friend, Maggie Bennett."

She supposed those words were as good as any. She wasn't his wife, or his fiancée. And he certainly couldn't introduce her as his lover.

She sighed, starting to worry about the wisdom of coming to this meeting, after all. It had seemed like a good idea this morning. She and Tate had finally cleared up everything with the police and he'd phoned his brother to set up the meeting. Then they'd gone shopping for new clothes at Phipps Plaza and checked into the Ritz Carlton, where Tate had his beard shaved and his hair restored to blond again.

Both of them had still been flying high on adrenaline then. But now, when she'd had time to settle down... She really shouldn't be here. She didn't belong. Maybe she should leave now, before the meeting started.

Then a man and a woman came into the room and it was too late for her to leave. Maggie would have known both of them were related to Tate, even if she hadn't been expecting them.

His mother was smaller and younger-looking than Maggie had imagined she would be. She was also prettier...except for her eyes, which were puffy. Probably from crying.

Maggie watched Elaine Rabun rush across the room to embrace Tate, who seemed embarrassed by his mother's show of emotion. He glanced at Maggie. She made a motion of encouragement with her head and, after a moment, Tate put his arms around his mother. Maggie smiled her approval.

She held her breath when she saw Tate's brother approach him, too. Brian's hair was sandy rather than blond, and he was a couple of inches shorter than Tate. Other than that, the two of them looked very much alike.

Brian extended his hand. Tate hesitated. Then he shook hands with his brother. Maggie let out the breath she'd been holding. After a moment, Tate glanced at Maggie again. She winked at him.

"LET'S GET right down to business," Tate said after calling the meeting to order. "First of all, I apologize for any worry or inconvenience my disappearance might have caused all of you. However, I felt it was necessary for me to drop out of sight for a time in order to make certain inquiries. As you all know, I had serious misgivings about merging the SCFC with Midsouth Investment Company."

"Don't tell us you're still harping on that!" Brian said.

"That's exactly what I'm telling you," Tate said.

"Can't you get it through your head that you lost that battle? We voted on it and won. It's over. Settled."

"I still haven't signed the merger papers," Tate pointed out. "And I don't intend to sign them."

"Dammit, Tate! You have to!" Brian shouted, getting to his feet.

"I don't have to do a damn thing. And I'll remind you that until you vote me out, I'm still president of this outfit. So shut up and sit back down, Brian."

Brian sat.

"Now where was I?" Tate said.

"You were rehashing all your old objections to Midsouth Investment Company," one of the board members said.

"Thank you for reminding me, Ben. And it turns out that my misgivings were more than justified." Tate patted a stack of folders lying on the table in front of him. "Midsouth Investment Company—your precious financial consortium, Brian—is nothing but a bunch of crooks."

Everybody started talking at once.

"You can't just make up things like that!"

"They'll sue us all for slander."

"Stop being a sore loser, Tate."

"Order! Order!" Tate kept shouting. "Now listen to me," he said when the noise finally died down. "I have proof right here to back up everything I say." He patted the folders again.

"First of all, the chicken processing plant that Midsouth was supposed to own in Panama City, Florida...they don't own it at all. The same holds true for the other plant they told us they owned in Birmingham. I have sworn affidavits, notarized, setting it all out."

"There must be some mistake," Brian said.

"There's no mistake, except the one you made when you believed what Midsouth told you."

"No," Brian insisted, shaking his head. "I saw papers."

"At one time, Midsouth did hold an option on both plants. You probably saw copies of those. They obtained those options by lying to the Garvey brothers, the real owners of the plants. But that's another story.

"The point is, the options that Midsouth held on the two processing plants have expired. They expired several months ago, I might add, way before the consortium entered into serious negotiations with you, Brian."

"I still can't believe it," Brian said.

"It's all here in black and white," Tate commented. "Let's face it. Those so-called big city 'gentlemen' have deliberately lied to us and tried to deceive us in every way possible. They obviously took the whole lot of us for a bunch of hillbillies."

Tate looked at Brian. Seeing his brother's stricken face and sickly pallor, he almost felt sorry for him. Almost.

"What do we do now, Tate?" Ben asked.

"Yeah," another board member said. "What *do* we do? They got us over a barrel for sure, don't they?"

Tate kept quiet, letting his board stew in its own juices for a while longer. "Well," he said finally. "I never did get around to signing those merger papers. I imagine it'll be simple enough for us to just call the whole thing off, especially when we show Midsouth copies of these sworn affidavits that prove they deliberately lied to us."

Tate could almost hear the collective sigh of relief that went around the room.

"Dang! You saved us that time, Tate!"

"Nice piece of work!"

"When will you talk to Midsouth, Tate?"

"Not me," Tate said. "I think we should leave it to Brian to tell them the good news."

Brian nodded sheepishly.

Tate savored his moment of triumph a little longer before he spoke again. "There's still one more item of business. I think my brother rushed into this Midsouth thing a little too fast. But I also think maybe I've been a little too cautious, as well. Maybe it *is* a good time for us to expand . . . but slowly, and with prudence.

"With that in mind, I talked with both the Garvey brothers at some length." He picked up one of the folders from the table. "And I signed an intent-to-purchase agreement with Lloyd Garvey at the Panama City plant. I also have first option on the Birmingham plant.

"I think this would be a good expansion move for the SCFC. But if you don't agree, I'm prepared to step down from the co-op and follow through with the purchase on my own, using my own savings. It's up to you whether or not you want me to continue at the SCFC, and whether you want to do business with me."

"We're with you, Tate!"

"All the way!"

"Anything you say!"

They took a vote and it was unanimous.

Tate—who had deliberately avoided looking in Maggie's direction during the battle—finally did. She was smiling at him. Her eyes were glistening with tears.

LATER, with his arm draped possessively around Maggie's shoulder, he introduced her to his family. Brian, more ill at ease than Tate had ever seen him before, apologized to Tate, to Maggie, to Tate again, and then excused himself to go make a phone call to Midsouth Investment Company.

"I guess it's my turn to apologize," Elaine said after Brian left.

"Only if you want to," Tate said quietly.

"I do want to. I'm sorry, Tate. Truly sorry to have put you through all this . . . making you so unhappy that you felt you had to leave town."

"I didn't exactly run away from home, Mom. I went out to prove something."

"And you did. I'm glad for that."

"Thank you." Tate felt Maggie nudge him in the ribs. "There's something I have to ask you, Mom," he said. "You don't have to answer, but I'd really like to know." He swallowed. "Why did you vote with Brian on the merger? And vote against me?"

"I didn't vote against you! I'd never do that."

"That's the way it came out, as far as I could see."

"I was trying to help you, Tate. Because you're just like your daddy was."

"I don't understand."

"You're serious, the same way he was. Way too serious, by far. And you're hardworking like he was. Your daddy worked and worried himself to death at an early age. I didn't want the same thing to happen to you."

"But how would your going along with Brian's scheme change things, except to put him in control of the company instead of me?"

"Brian's not serious the way you are, and I never worried about him the way I do you. You've worked hard all your life, since you were still a child. Brian told me that he'd like to take some of the worry off your shoulders for a change."

"Sure," Tate said sarcastically. "He'd like to take the whole . . ." He stopped when Maggie nudged him. Hard. "So that's why you went along with him?" he said instead.

"As God is my witness," his mother vowed with tears in her eyes.

Maggie nudged Tate again, not so hard as before. He put his arms around his mother and hugged her.

"I learned a lesson, though," Elaine said.

"What's that?" Tate asked.

"I thought that all of Brian's schooling would have made him smarter than he's turned out to be. He's still wet behind the ears as far as I'm concerned. Don't you dare let him take over things around here!"

"I have no intention of letting him," Tate said with a laugh.

"SEE? I TOLD YOU your mother probably had a good reason for what she did," Maggie said much later when they were alone in their hotel room. Several members of the board, including Elaine, had tried to talk them into going out to celebrate after the meeting but Tate had declined, pleading exhaustion after almost no sleep for three days and two nights.

"Yes," Tate agreed. "She was way off base in what she did, but she did it for the right reasons. Brian's another story. He was blind, greedy, following his own selfish ambition."

"Can you ever forgive him?"

"Possibly. Somewhere down the line. After all, he's still my brother and I love him. But I'll never forget. And I'll never completely trust him again."

Maggie thought about that. She sighed. "I'm glad you shook hands with him, at least. For your mom's sake."

"Sentimental Maggie," he chided, walking over to stand beside her at the window, which looked out onto Peachtree Road in the heart of Buckhead.

"I'm not ashamed of it," she said defensively.

"There's no reason why you should be," he said, pushing back a tendril of hair from her cheek, then letting his fingers linger there. "You have every reason to be proud of it."

"Now you're making fun of me," she said, wondering if she was trying to pick a fight with him.

He wondered if she was trying to pick a fight with him. If so, he wasn't biting. Fighting was the very last thing on earth he wanted to do with Maggie. Especially now, when time was so precious because they'd probably be saying goodbye to each other soon. Any day now. Any hour.

"I'm not making fun of you, Maggie. I love the way you are—full of life and love...and...and everything." He stopped because his throat closed up on him. But there was so much more he wanted to say to her.

Maggie wished he hadn't stopped. There were so many more words she wanted to hear. So many more she wanted to say to him.

"I, uh, guess you'll be going back to work right away," she said.

"I thought I'd take a couple more days off to rest." Resting was the last thing he wanted to do. He wanted to spend every moment of their remaining time together with Maggie, wide-awake, storing up memories for the long, lonely years ahead.

"I thought...I mean, I'd hoped we could spend them here together," he said. "We could relax in luxury for a change. But you might have made other plans..."

"Me? No. But this place has to be expensive as all get-out."

"I can afford it. And I'd like us to stay here, Maggie. After some of the places we've stayed, you certainly deserve it." She did deserve it, and he wanted to give it to her, although he'd have preferred that they spend their last time together at his A-frame cabin on Lake Lanier.

She'd personally have preferred to spend their remaining time at his place—soaking up memories, sentimental sap that she was. But if Tate wanted the impersonal atmosphere of a hotel, even one as luxurious as this was, she wasn't going to argue with him. She'd stay with him anyplace he wanted... for as long as he wanted.

"Well, okay," she said. "This is very nice of you, Tate."

Nice? he thought. This was what the two of them had come to... all that was left between them? He remembered the dangers they'd faced together. The challenges. The bond they'd shared. And it all boiled down to... *nice?*

"I thought you'd like it," he said.

"I do."

"You sure could have fooled me."

"What do you expect me to do? Fall on my knees and kiss your feet?"

This is more like it! he thought, getting ready to do battle with her. "A simple thank you would have been quite sufficient."

Okay, she thought. Now they were getting somewhere—down to nitty-gritty emotions, the way she'd been aching to do. "I already told you that."

"No. You said this was 'nice.' Which could mean almost anything."

"In this case, it meant almost nothing."

"Aha! Then why did you say it?"

"Because I didn't want to hurt your feelings! Okay?"

"Not okay! We agreed a long time ago that we'd be honest with each other. Remember?"

"I remember. And how about you, Tate? Have you been honest with me?"

"Yes!"

"Completely honest?"

"Yes!" He stopped. Thought about his answer again. "Well . . . almost completely."

"What haven't you told me? That you can hardly wait for me to get out of here? That you're so anxious to be rid of me that you'd rather stay cooped up at a lousy hotel rather than take the risk of showing me where you live?"

Her charges were so ridiculous, he didn't know where to begin. "Lousy hotel?" he said, settling on one.

"I'll withdraw lousy. But it's still a hotel."

Tate had never had a migraine in his life, but thought he might be on the brink of one now. He took a deep breath. "Maggie, the time I wasn't honest with you was when I told you I cared for you."

She stopped breathing. Her heart skipped a beat.

"Those words don't begin to describe the way I feel about you. I don't merely care about you, Maggie. I love you."

Her heart skipped another beat. Luckily for her, she had a really healthy heart, and it started pounding again almost immediately. Double time. "You love me?" she repeated.

"Yes. And not only that. I absolutely, totally adore you. I'm sorry."

"I'm not," she said, moving a cautious step toward him. "Not in the least. Because I love and absolutely, totally adore you, too." She forgot caution and flung her arms around his neck, trying to pull his head down so she could kiss him.

He fought her off.

It was a valiant fight, but he lost. Or won. At this stage, he wasn't sure which it was.

"This doesn't change things, Maggie," he said, finally managing to disengage his lips from hers.

"Of course it does," she said, trying to kiss him again.

"No!" he shouted, pulling her arms from around his neck and stepping back out of her reach. "I won't do it."

Maggie blinked in total confusion. "Do what?"

"I won't stand in the way of your career. My life is here in Atlanta, Maggie...certainly for the next few years while we go through this expansion. I owe it to the SCFC to follow through on it."

"Of course you do. I wouldn't expect you to do otherwise."

"And I can't expect you to bury yourself here, to throw away your hopes and dreams, everything you've worked for..."

She suddenly grinned. "So that's it."

"What?"

"You know something, Tate? You're a romantic, after all. Even if you won't admit it."

"What are you talking about?"

"You're willing to give me up—the woman you say you love..."

"I *do* love you!"

"But you're prepared to give me up for a dream. My dream. If that's not being a romantic, I don't know what is."

Tate didn't know what to say to that. She seemed to have him dead to rights.

"I love you all the more for that, Tate. But you don't know much about the recording business, do you?"

"Well...no. I never claimed to—"

"If you did, you'd know there's a lot more to it than singing on a stage or in a studio in Nashville."

"What are you getting at?"

"If I do succeed, and that's still not a certainty..."

"I'm sure of it."

"Thanks." She smiled. "If I do succeed, I'll want to write my own songs and do my own arrangements, which I can do anywhere. And Nashville doesn't have a monopoly on recording studios, either. There are some highly professional, respected studios in a lot of cities, including Atlanta."

"Oh?"

"Yes. And even though some of the superstars live in Nashville, it's mainly because that's where they want to live. Other stars choose other places. Alan Jackson lives in Newnan, only a short drive south of here. And Travis Tritt lives in Marietta, which you can see out the window of this hotel on a clear day."

Tate grinned. "I think I'm beginning to get the picture."

"If I'm a success..."

"I wish you'd stop saying, 'if.'"

"Okay. *When* I'm a success, I'll probably need to go to Nashville occasionally. But how many flights a day do you suppose operate between here and there?"

"I don't know. Do you?"

"No. But I'm sure it's lots. And it's only a fifty-minute flight, for heaven's sake."

"For that matter," Tate said, catching Maggie's enthusiasm, "I've been thinking about buying a company plane, now that we'll have plants in Panama City and Birmingham."

Maggie narrowed her eyes. "How long have you been thinking about buying a company plane?"

"A long time. At least ten seconds."

"So what other excuses do you have not to make an honest woman out of me?"

"None," he said, laughing as he scooped her up in his arms. "We really *can* have it all! Your career." He kissed her. "My career." He kissed her again. "And a life together at the same time!" He scattered kisses all over her face. "Will you marry me, Maggie Bennett?" he asked between kisses.

She kissed him back. "Happily, Tate Rabun," she answered, laughing along with him. "Happily ever after."

MEN MADE IN AMERICA

Fifty red-blooded, white-hot, true-blue hunks
from every State in the Union!

Look for MEN MADE IN AMERICA! Written by some
of our most poplar authors, these stories feature fifty of
the strongest, sexiest men, each from a different state in
the union!

Two titles available every other month at your favorite
retail outlet.

In November, look for:

STRAIGHT FROM THE HEART by Barbara Delinsky
(Connecticut)
AUTHOR'S CHOICE by Elizabeth August (Delaware)

In January, look for:

DREAM COME TRUE by Ann Major (Florida)
WAY OF THE WILLOW by Linda Shaw (Georgia)

You won't be able to resist MEN MADE IN AMERICA!

HARLEQUIN CELEBRATES
THE SEASON OF SHARING
AND FAMILY WITH

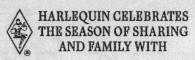

Friends, Families,
Lovers

Harlequin introduces the latest member in its family of
seasonal collections. Following in the footsteps of the popular
My Valentine, Just Married and *Harlequin Historical Christmas
Stories,* we are proud to present FRIENDS, FAMILIES,
LOVERS. A collection of three new contemporary romance
stories about America at its best, about welcoming others into
the circle of love.... Stories to warm your heart ...

By three leading romance authors:

KATHLEEN EAGLE
SANDRA KITT
RUTH JEAN DALE

Available in October, wherever
Harlequin books are sold.

1993 Keepsake

CHRISTMAS

Stories

Capture the spirit and romance of Christmas with KEEPSAKE CHRISTMAS STORIES, a collection of three stories by favorite historical authors. The perfect Christmas gift!

Don't miss these heartwarming stories, available in November wherever Harlequin books are sold:

ONCE UPON A CHRISTMAS by Curtiss Ann Matlock
A FAIRYTALE SEASON by Marianne Willman
TIDINGS OF JOY by Victoria Pade

ADD A TOUCH OF ROMANCE TO YOUR HOLIDAY SEASON WITH KEEPSAKE CHRISTMAS STORIES!

HX93

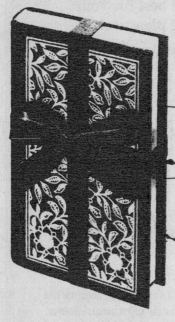